WHODUNNIT?

ALAN RADNOR

Ten original short detection stories of mystery and murder written closely to the format of the long-running Whodunnit? television series.

ITV Books/Arrow

for
Zoe Jane-the greatest
mystery of them all

WHODUNNIT?

by
ALAN RADNOR

Introduction by
JON PERTWEE

Illustrations by
TONY STREEK

ITV Books/Arrow

Jointly published by
INDEPENDENT TELEVISION BOOKS LTD
247 Tottenham Court Road, London W1P 0AU

and

ARROW BOOKS LTD
3 Fitzroy Square, London W1

An imprint of the Hutchinson Publishing Group

London Melbourne Sydney Auckland Wellington Johannesburg and agencies throughout the world

First published, 1978

Set in VIP Baskerville Medium 10/11 pt

ISBN: 0 09 919070 2

Printed in Great Britain by Anchor Press Ltd, Tiptree, Essex

CONTENTS

INTRODUCTION BY JON PERTWEE

All crimes are solved by a mixture of luck, skill and good detection. In these clever pieces of false trailing by Alan Radnor, the most sleuthful and ardent detectives among you may well be hard pressed to spot the clues and sort the mysteries and criminals from the red herrings and innocents.

The major crime of murder is mainly committed in the heat of the moment by the person most familiar to the victim – father, mother, lover and so on. In these short stories, greed and self-protection are the primary motivators in a series of bizarre yet realistic, if not artful, crimes from grand robbery to murder most foul.

As in my television series the sketches here are not primarily concerned with the consequence or motivation of the criminal involved. They are concerned with the way even the most carefully thought out alibi or defence may be efficiently dismembered by detailed and logical detective work. Desperate men take desperate measures, which, fortunately for any detective, often lead to desperate mistakes being made. However these mistakes often rest in the commonplace and it needs sharp ears and eyes to spot them.

Included in most of the stories is an illustration of a scene from the crime. In this way small, but often important, visual clues are provided which should help your detective work. Be careful though – not all the clues are useful, many are pure red herrings.

As a curious nation we are all intrigued by acts involving death and suicide and there is a full range of highly suspicious deaths in the following stories. Don't jump to conclusions too early though — accidents do happen and sometimes accidents can be made to happen.

You will have to think of yourself not only as detective, but as judge or coroner in these matters. Sort the valid from the superfluous and nobble your man!

There have, of course, been many famous detectives in fiction, many of whom I would thoroughly enjoy playing in full deerstalking and cloak swirling glory. But one of my favourites must surely be Agatha Christie's Miss Marple.

I can see it now — the night is cold, dark and menacing. The lonely figure of a woman stalks silently in the shadows, past the church gateway, swiftly across the unmade road, armed nobly with hatpin and stout walking stick. Slowly her figure becomes clear as she looms through the mist under the light of a flickering gas lamp. The background music reaches its peak as she turns to show her face . . . We know, they whisper . . . it's Margaret Rutherford. Good Lord! they gasp . . . it's Jon Pertwee!
Well . . . why not?

Anyway, I wish you happy reading with the Whodunnit book of short stories and most of all happy detecting to you all.

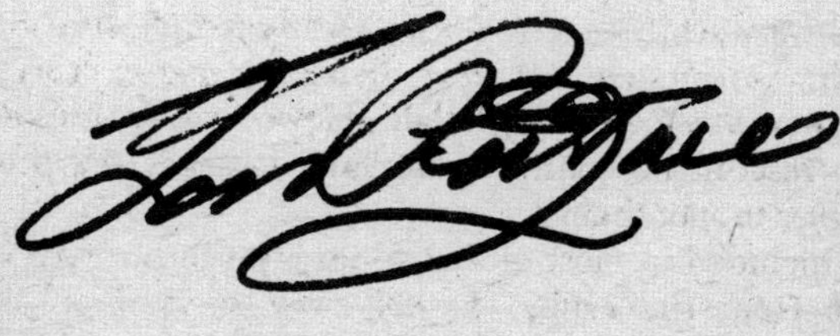

A CASE OF SUICIDE?

'This is what you British call a busman's holiday, I think,' said Monsieur Mollé without humour to the small group gathered in the greenhouse of Sir Michael Forsyth. The famous French detective shivered in the chill of early dawn and gazed once again at the body of Sir Michael lying sprawled on a deck chair before him.

Mollé had been wakened five minutes earlier by Sir Michael's butler and told of the discovery. Dressing quickly, he had hurried down with the butler to the greenhouse where Sir Michael lay. Two other house guests of the weekend party were already there—Dr Stanley Jenkins, the family doctor and friend of Sir Michael, and Algernon Blythe, the nephew of the deceased man. The head gardener, Tom Black, who had been the one to discover the body, was also present.

Although distressed at the sight of his old friend lying dead, Mollé nonetheless pulled himself together quickly.

'Someone must call the police,' he ordered, nodding at the butler who scurried off. 'In the meanwhile I suggest we return to the library. Let us wake the other guests and, as I am somewhat used to this, I shall try to help your police by finding out as much as I can from you all before they come.'

'It seems like an obvious case of suicide to me, Monsieur Mollé,' said Algernon Blythe.

'Perhaps so, perhaps not,' the detective commented.

'I remember the case of Jacques Broussant . . . but that is for another time. Tell me, Mr Black, everything here is as you found it, no?'

'Exactly sir,' the gardener replied, twisting his cap nervously in his hands. 'I comes here just after six this morning to get some bedding plants out and finds Sir Michael just as you sees him.'

Mollé grunted and looked at the body once more. Sir Michael lay sprawled on the deck chair, his legs straight out in front of him. His left hand dangled at his side, while his right lay across his lap. On the ground beside him lay an automatic pistol, and two feet in front of him lay a spent cartridge, to the left of his feet. At Sir Michael's right temple an ugly gun-shot wound showed where the bullet had entered, killing him instantly. A trickle of dried blood had run down from the wound, staining the white collar of his shirt. A dark tie hung loosely over the dead man's waistcoat.

'Correct me if I'm wrong,' Mollé said to Blythe and Dr Jenkins. 'But wasn't Sir Michael wearing a large diamond tie-pin last night at dinner?'

'Good heavens, I think you're right!' the doctor gasped. 'It's not there now. You don't think someone pinched it and then killed Michael to make it look as if it was suicide?'

'Perhaps, perhaps,' the detective muttered. 'We shall see. But it is most curious, would you not agree?'

Blythe and Jenkins nodded slowly.

'Well, we shall find out more back at the house,' said Mollé grimly. 'Oh, by the way Mr Black, let me congratulate you on a most excellently stocked greenhouse. Being a bit of an amateur gardener myself, I appreciate such things. But tell me, does not that broken window beside Sir Michael upset your temperature control?' he asked, pointing to a grimy pane of glass to the right of the deck chair.

'I've been meaning to fix that thing for ages, sir,' the gardener chuckled. 'I can see you're a detective. But as it so happens it doesn't bother the plants at all. Mind you,

with the seedlings coming up as they are now, it'll have to be fixed, what with the window facing north-west and getting them winds.'

Mollé and the gardener chatted about gardening on the way back to the main house. The detective then asked the butler to gather all the other house guests in the library. As well as Blythe and Jenkins, Spencer McNee, the actor, and Robert Carstairs, a business partner of Sir Michael, were now sitting around the large, book-filled room. The butler told Mollé that the police would be arriving in about twenty minutes—'The house is rather far from the nearest town,' he added by way of excuse when he saw Mollé's look of surprise — and then suggested organising coffee and sandwiches for the group.

'An excellent idea,' the Frenchman nodded. 'I can see why you butlers are in such demand — you know how to cope with every situation. A wonderful English tradition, the butler,' he beamed.

A large pot of coffee and some sandwiches appeared, and Mollé settled back in the large, winged leather chair he was sitting in.

'I'm sure you do not mind me asking you a few questions. My old friend Sir Michael would have approved. And there *is* the question of the missing tie-pin.'

The four others shook their heads silently.

'Let us take the events in sequence,' said Mollé, smiling, 'for I am a logical man. Dr Jenkins, you were the first to see the body after the gardener's discovery, were you not?' he inquired.

'That's correct,' Jenkins replied. 'The butler woke me around 6.45 and I rushed to the greenhouse. Well, you know what I found. I estimated that the death had taken place about four or five hours earlier.'

'And you would say without doubt that the cause of death was a bullet through the brain?'

'Without an autopsy, I would say most definitely. . .'

'Excuse me, sir,' the butler interrupted, coming through the door with an envelope in his hand. 'This was found on Sir Michael's desk.' He handed the envelope to

Mollé.

The detective carefully opened it, making sure to keep his fingers at the very edge. He pulled out a sheet of white paper and read the note aloud:

> *'Tonight is the last night of my life. Dr Jenkins has just told me that I am suffering from cancer and there is very little hope. I cannot go on, especially as my wife died of the same disease only a few years ago. Everyone is waiting for me to die – my nephew, who does not think it, but will receive most of my estate; my business partner, Robert Carstairs, who finds me a nuisance; and even my penniless old friend, who knows he will receive some money when I die because he saved my life during the war. So all in all, it is better for me to die with some dignity.'*

There was silence in the library after Mollé had read the note. The detective looked across at Dr Jenkins.

'Is this true?' he asked. 'Sir Michael was dying of cancer?'

'I'm afraid so,' Jenkins sighed. 'He had been for a while. At first it was thought he could be operated on, but some tests we did last week showed it was only a matter of time.'

'When did you tell Sir Michael this?' Mollé inquired.

'Last night after dinner,' replied the doctor.

'But Sir Michael went to bed after dinner,' Mollé protested.

'He went to his bedroom, Monsieur Mollé,' said the doctor, correcting him. 'In fact, he called for me about two hours later and complained he couldn't sleep. I suggested he went for a walk and offered to go with him. Normally I gave him a mild sleeping pill, but I decided not to last night. Well, we walked towards the greenhouse, and it was then that I told him about his illness.'

'What was his reaction then?'

'That's the funny part of it,' Jenkins answered, looking puzzled. 'He seemed to take it quite calmly. All he said was that it had been a good job he had changed his will.'

'Oh, yes?' commented Mollé. 'And did you know about this will?'

'As a matter of fact, yes. I was a witness to it, you see. It was well known that the only heir to the fortune was Algernon, with whom Sir Michael did not get on very well. For years Sir Michael had been saying he would make sure Algernon would not inherit. I'm sure I'm not breaking any confidences when I say that Sir Michael drew up another will on Friday which actually gave Algernon the bulk of the estate.'

Sir Michael's nephew gasped in surprise, but Jenkins continued.

'On Saturday morning Sir Michael's lawyers arrived with the papers — before any of you had reached here — and I was asked to be a witness. It was then that Sir Michael told me about Algernon. But shortly before dinner, he asked me into his study. The two of us sat there and discussed this and that for about ten minutes, and I was beginning to wonder why he had wanted to see me. Then he told me he had made some further changes in the will and needed me to be a witness to make it legal. He refused to tell me what changes he had put in, so I just put my signature on the paper and left to change for dinner. No doubt the butler will confirm that I was with Sir Michael.'

'No need to,' Mollé said. 'I myself saw you come out of Sir Michael's study about fifteen minutes before dinner. But one more thing, Dr Jenkins. What were you treating Sir Michael for apart from his cancer?'

'It was well known that he had a weak heart,' Jenkins said. 'And he'd had a couple of attacks recently.'

'He couldn't have died from a heart attack then?'

'What? In the time it takes a bullet to pass through the brain? Hardly, Monsieur. And I think even a great detective like yourself would find it difficult to believe that a man who'd had a stroke would then shoot himself.'

'Quite, quite,' the detective smiled. 'You are a most observant and logical man, Dr Jenkins. You would have made a good detective.'

'Well as a matter of fact I do write short detective stories for magazines,' said the doctor, proudly. 'Perhaps we may speak about that later.'

Mollé clapped his hands together. 'I thought so! We have two detective minds here,' he laughed. 'I will be grateful for any help you may offer, Dr Jenkins. But I have one last question. Where did you leave Sir Michael after giving him the terrible news?'

'In the greenhouse,' the doctor replied. 'I felt tired and went back to the house. As you will remember, there was a thunder storm about to break and the sky was black. The first drops of rain actually began to fall as I reached the lawn outside the front. I met Algernon there and cracked a joke about needing an umbrella if he was going walking.'

'Thank you, doctor, you've been most helpful. I certainly look forward to our future chats.'

He turned next to Algernon Blythe. 'Mr Blythe, a strange question first of all. Why is it that your hair is all curled and tousled this morning, when last night it was swept straight back?'

'I. . . I. . . I washed it last night,' Blythe said in surprise. 'This always happens unless I blow-dry it, which I'll do later.'

'Thank you. Where did you go after seeing Dr Jenkins on the lawn last night?'

'I was walking towards the greenhouse, when the rain began to fall pretty heavily. I raced the last bit and got under cover just before it began pouring.'

'And your uncle was there?'

'Yes, he was standing by that deckchair we found him in, looking very serious. I told him he could catch his death of cold on a night like that, and he swung on me and began shouting.'

'What prompted that, Mr Blythe?'

'He said I would be glad to see him dead because I thought I was inheriting all his money,' Blythe said quietly. 'He called me a waster, and said it was time I earned some money of my own. I reminded him I had a good job in the City, but it made no difference. You see, I think he'd always been upset that he'd had no children of his own. Anyway, he ranted on and said I wasn't even worth the tie-pin he was wearing. He pulled his tie out, snatched the pin off and flung it at me, but it fell on the ground among some plants.'

'Ah, so the mystery of the tie-pin is solved!' Mollé exclaimed. 'But what provoked this sudden outburst last night?'

'Oh, I don't know,' Algernon sighed. 'After dinner, you'll remember, he went to his room. About half-an-hour later, the butler asked me to go up and see my uncle. When I got there, he hinted to me that he had made certain changes in his will which could be to my advantage, but only if I showed more interest in family affairs. He was always saying that about my interest, but quite honestly, he never told me anything about his business and the running of the estates. So I couldn't help him.'

'Ah, yes, Sir Michael always was one to do things on his own,' agreed the detective. 'So when did you leave the greenhouse?'

'When the rain died down a bit.'

'But the storm went on most of the night,' said the detective. 'I remember being wakened about four o'clock by a thunder clap and hearing the rain against my window.'

'Yes, but I found a polythene bag and I dashed to the house with the bag over my head. Unfortunately, some earth fell off it and landed on my hair, which was why I washed it last night.'

The Frenchman said nothing for a few moments. He gazed at Algernon Blythe.

'You do realise you are now a very wealthy young man?' he said finally, in a quiet voice.

'Yes, but I wouldn't kill for money!' Blythe protested, looking like an outraged schoolboy.

'I didn't say you would,' observed Mollé calmly. 'Now, I'd like to ask Mr Carstairs a few questions. You and Sir Michael were business partners, I gather. But things were not well between you. Why?'

Robert Carstairs stared at the detective for a few seconds before answering.

'To tell the truth, Mr Mollé, I took Sir Michael in with me because of his title and connections. He was meant to be a sleeping partner, but he wouldn't blinking well lie down. He kept poking his nose in where he had no business and ruined a couple of good contracts. I'd told him only yesterday afternoon that I was going to call an Extraordinary General Meeting and expose his uselessness and then I was going to have him voted off the board.'

'How did he take that?'

'Told me to go to hell.'

'And you didn't discuss it with him further?'

'No. After dinner he went up to his room. You remember you and I played some cards and then I went upstairs. As I was passing his room I heard this shouting match between him and Algernon. I didn't take much notice and went straight to bed. The next thing I know is being wakened this morning and told to come here.'

'And you never went out at all after dinner?'

'Never moved from the house.'

'Very well. That leaves you Mr McNee,' said Mollé, glancing at the actor. 'What did *you* do last night after dinner?'

'I. . . I. . . achoo!' McNee sneezed. 'Excuse me, but I seem to have caught a cold,' he said. 'I was out in that bloody storm last night. I'd gone out for a run around the grounds — part of my keep-fit programme, you know— when it began to pour.'

'That is terrible, but I would have thought a bath after your run would have helped,' Mollé said sympathetically.

'I had a bath. It wasn't the rain that gave me the cold. It was that freezing westerly wind. So much for trying to keep fit!' he moaned.

'I am sure Mr Carstairs' medical state isn't going to help answer any of your questions, Monsieur Mollé,' said Dr Jenkins sarcastically. 'From what I've heard it's an obvious suicide, and we have the note to prove it now.'

'Ah, you amateur detectives,' smiled Mollé. 'You make our job very hard, you know. Mr Carstairs, where did you go for your run?'

'Down across the lawn, round the back of the greenhouse and up the side to the orchards on the west side of the house. That's where I got my cold,' he added, shooting a glance at Dr Jenkins.

'So you passed the greenhouse?'

'Twice,' the actor said. 'The first time on the way to the field at the back I saw Algernon talking to Sir Michael, and the next time Dr Jenkins was there.'

'And then you came straight back to the house?'

'Yes, via the orchards as I've said. Then I had a bath and went straight to bed.'

'Thank you, Mr Carstairs.'

Mollé looked at the suicide note in front of him. 'It says here you would benefit from the will and that you are penniless. Is this true?'

'I'm afraid so, Monsieur,' the actor replied. 'The acting profession is hardly full of millionaires. At the moment I'm pretty desperate if truth be known. So when Sir Michael told me last night before dinner that he would be leaving me something in his will, I was of course very pleased. At least I could tell my bank manager something would be coming my way eventually. Although I'm not exactly pleased the way it happened.'

The detective shifted in his seat and closed his eyes. After a few minutes he opened them and stared round at the four men.

'It is a most interesting case,' he said. 'Mr Blythe, Mr Carstairs and Mr McNee have very good reasons for wanting to see the death of Sir Michael. But one of you gentlemen is lying to me. You see, Sir Michael was murdered, and. . .,' he paused and glanced at his watch, 'when the police arrive in a few minutes, I will be able to tell them who to arrest—or is it whom to arrest. You must excuse my English,' he smiled. 'Although the crime was cleverly done, there is no such thing as the perfect murder. The criminal is nearly always found out. As we French say, *C'est la vie*—or in this case, *C'est la mort!*'

So–whodunnit? Turn to the back of the book and check your detective work with Mollé's observations.

A CURSE ON THE PHARAOH'S ROD

The Egyptian Government had not been at all happy about allowing the newly-discovered relics from the tomb of Akmenon to be exhibited in London; but the archaeological expedition had been financed jointly by Britain and Egypt, so they had little choice. However, when the most treasured item—the Golden Sceptre of the Pharaoh, said to have been handed down by the god Horus—was stolen, there was very nearly a break in diplomatic relations between the two countries.

Fortunately, the man in charge of the investigation was Chief Superintendent Peter Brownlee, who managed to find the sceptre after only two days of interviewing everyone involved. The Superintendent tells his own story:

'I was alerted at 2.30 am on the morning of April 17, 19—. When I reached the museum, I found the side door next to the main entrance open. All the lights were on in the building, and I was met in the hall by the two guards, Arthur Mason and John Mackay. Professor Bartholomew was also present, but in a very distressed state. I proceeded immediately to the exhibition room, where I found the glass case which had housed the Golden Sceptre hanging open.

'I made my way to the Guard Room where I took statements from the three men present, recording them on tape, while Detective Sergeant Wilson got ready to take fingerprints in the Exhibition Room. (It later became apparent that there were no fingerprints.) It soon became clear that I would have to question a further three men—the two guards who had gone off duty at 10 am the previous night and an Egyptian gentleman by the name of Ahmid. It was Ahmid who had actually placed the sceptre in the case, his role being that of representative of the Egyptian Government.

'After arranging for these three other gentlemen to be called to the museum, I took statements from them too. After comparing these with the other statements and questioning them all again collectively, and allowing a day to check alibis, I was able to pinpoint the culprit and make an arrest.

'The statements (in the order in which I recorded them) were as follows:

Professor K. J. Bartholomew, MAHons(Cantab) FRCA

"I accompanied the sceptre and other antiquities over from Egypt. There were two separate journeys, because of the number and size of relics found. The sceptre was part of the second load. As you know, it had been decided to use an 'overspill' museum in Kensington for part of the exhibition, as the British Museum did not have enough space available. It was to this second museum that the sceptre was taken, and put in place only yesterday.

"I must admit that I did not like that fellow Ahmid from the start. I mean, he was completely against anything being taken out of Egypt for show abroad, and deeply resented the fact that our own government had partly sponsored the dig in the first place. And then he kept going on about all this superstitious nonsense, getting the wind up practically everyone.

"He wouldn't stop rabbiting on until the very end, you know. For example, as we were putting the sceptre in the show case, he told me that the Golden Rod should never have been taken from the tomb at all.

"Well, I saw red. I was the one who had discovered the tomb, buried under the desert sands, and I'm not being immodest when I say, as I have said before, that I believe this is only the first of many such finds. There must be hundreds of treasures under these sands, if only we were allowed to dig for them without all this political nonsense.

"I'm sorry, I digress. As I say, Ahmid and I made sure that the sceptre was securely placed in the show-case yesterday. There were two guards in the room, which had no other cases in it. They were Peter Haskins and Alex Brown, both of whom I have known for many years.

" 'This should have never been taken from the tomb,' I remember Ahmid saying. 'The curse will be sure to follow.' He held the sceptre away from him as if it was a bomb about to explode.

"That's when I lost my temper, I'm afraid. I suppose it was reaction to the weeks of nonsense I'd heard from him. I accused him of being a stupid, superstitious scare-monger, and implied that it was people like him who created mysteries by making sure disaster did follow. Then I told him the sceptre was going to stay in this country long enough for the experts to examine it and perhaps gain a clue into the whereabouts of the other hidden treasures.

"He looked at me, narrowed his eyes and sneered. Then without a word, he put the sceptre in the case, turned his back on us and walked out angrily. It was obvious I'd offended the fellow. That was the last I saw of him.

"I went upstairs to my office to catch up on the mountains of work which had collected during my absence. This was about 7.30 am, I think. I only left the office twice—once to go to the toilet and the second time to make a cup of tea in the kitchen beside the Guard Room. As I walked along the corridor I met a guard, whom I did not recognize but now know to be the temporary man, Arthur Mason. We didn't speak, and I went into the kitchen where I made my tea. I noticed that the time on the clock when I went in was twenty past two. I was amazed that I'd been working so long. I stayed in the kitchen about ten minutes making my tea and was heading back towards my office when the lights went out. Foolishly, I dropped my cup of tea and began running towards the main hall.

"I heard footsteps around me, and a door opening. I stumbled about for a few minutes and then the lights went back on, and I heard the alarm ringing. I rushed to the Guard Room, found the two guards, and we ran to the Exhibition Room, where we discovered the sceptre gone. I need not add what I felt, as I think I was still shocked when you arrived. And that's all I can tell you, Superintendent."

John Mackay, Guard

"I still can't take it in, mate. . . I mean, sir, twenty years working at the museum and not so much as a whisper. And then this. Cor, makes you think, dunnit? Mind you, I knew things were not going to be quiet as soon as I heard old Wally was in his sick bed. That's Walter Matthews, the other regular guard who was meant to be on night shift with me this month. There's three shifts, as you probably know. Six in the morning until two in the afternoon—we call that the tourist-trap shift, on account of all the coach loads that come. Then there's the two 'til ten shift—that's not too bad, what with the museum closing at six and just having to check and supervise any new stuff coming in. The last shift—the graveyard shift, we call it—is from ten at night through to six the next morning.

"So, as I say, Wally and me are up for the graveyard shift. I get this call from Wally late afternoon telling me he's down with food poisoning—mind you, with these sandwiches his old lady gives him, I'm not surprised—and I've to call Security Corps, the people who provide guards, for the name of the temporary man. That's how I meet Arthur Mason, and we decide it's best for me to meet him in *The Goose and Hare* before the shift starts and I'll take him along to the museum.

"So we get together and he seems a decent enough young bloke, and we chat about this and that. He asks me what's in the museum and I tell him about this here new exhibition. Well, we get here just before ten and Alex Brown lets us in. Alex is a stickler for form and insists on checking out young Mason's papers before he lets him step inside. Quite right, I suppose, in view of what's happened tonight.

"Anyway, you've seen the lay-out of the place, guv, so you know that next to our room is a walk-in cupboard with all the controls for the lights and burglar alarms. You only need to pull two switches and everything goes. We keep the cupboard locked and the key is kept in our room in a little glass case—that one over there on the wall beside the door. Blow me if I don't notice the key is missing when I get in on duty. So I go through to the locker rooms—that's them behind you, gov—where we change when we come on or go off shifts. I say to Peter—Peter Haskins, the other guard—the key's missing.

" 'Blimey,' he says, 'it's in my pocket. We were bringing in that glorified backscratcher tonight and I needed it to turn the bells off,' he tells me and gives me the key which I put back in its case.

"I show Arthur the kitchen and the lay-out of the place, and at eleven o'clock we make our first round. We do a tour every hour on the hour, y'see. Just before two, we get ready for our tour of inspection. I says to Arthur it's his turn to make the tea for when we get back and he says okay, he'll go straight to the kitchen and meet me in the Guard Room.

"I'm at the other side of the museum in the Prehistoric Section when my torch goes out. I sit and fiddle with it for about ten minutes, knowing I'd put new batteries in earlier in the night, when suddenly all the lights go out, and I'm left sitting in the black. Luckily I knew my way about, so I belt back to the main hall. I feel this draught of air and figure the door's open, and I hear someone stumbling about.

"I rush to the control cupboard, which I find open with the key in it, and knowing where the master switches are, I fling them on. The lights come back up and the bells start ringing. I lock the control cupboard and come back into our room to put the key back. I check the other keys quickly, but see none is missing.

"Well, it doesn't take me long to figure out what's been broken into—you see that big panel on the wall sir? Well, that's the lay-out of the museum and these little bulbs tell us if someone's tampering with the goods, so we can get there pretty sharpish. And as you know, the burglar alarms go direct to the police station five minutes away.

"Old Prof Bartholomew comes hoofing into the Guard Room with young Mason on his heels and we hightail it up to the Exhibition Room and find the sceptre gone. I thought the Prof was going to have a heart attack when he sees his precious rod gone. Arthur and me don't know what to do, so we comes back here and drinks the tea Arthur'd made. Then you turn up. And that's it from me."

Arthur Mason, Guard

"I'm fairly new to this game, and signed on with Security Corps only a year ago. It's a good living, and I'm not long married so I need the money. Right now, until I'm given a full-time position, I do relief work—you know, if someone is ill or on holiday.

"I get this call from the office yesterday telling me to report to the museum at ten last night. I'm told that John Mackay will be phoning me before, which he does and we meet in a pub, before coming on here.

"John shows me round, and after there's been a bit of a fuss over the control cupboard key, he tells me how the burglar alarm system operates. It's all very quiet, and John tells me about Prof Bartholomew who's working upstairs.

"'If you see him and he says nothing, don't get the hump,' he tells me. 'The Prof's like that with everyone. Lives in a world of his own,' he says.

"Well, I do run into the Prof after coming back from the two o'clock tour. He's walking along the corridor going to the kitchen and he meets me as I'm on my way back with two mugs of tea for John and me. True enough, he didn't even say hello. I get into the Guard Room expecting John to be there, and was surprised to find the place empty. I looked at the punch-out clock and see it's 2.20 am. I put the tea down on that little table over there and start to go out to look for John. I'm half-way up the corridor, trying to remember which sections John covered—we go in opposite directions, you understand—when the lights go out, and there's all this running around. I heard a crash and wondered what the hell was going on.

"The thing is, I'm like a blind man down an alley, not knowing my way about, and keep banging into statues and things. When the lights did go on again, I found myself in the museum shop, leading off the main hall. I made for the Guard Room and turned into the corridor where I saw Professor Bartholomew in front of me. We found John in the room and he tells us to get moving as there'd been a burglary. The rest you know."

Alex Brown, Guard

"There's not much I can tell you, I think. I supervised the placing of the sceptre in its case yesterday in accordance with the rules and regulations of the museum. I thought that Egyptian chap was a bit rude, but then again we're used to that—I don't blame them, I suppose, seeing us going across and taking their treasures away.

"Peter Haskins and I locked the case, and I checked the burglar alarm was connected. Professor Bartholomew watched us, although I thought he was a bit touchy after the foreigner started going on about the curse. Not that talk like that worries me—if we were to worry about every so-called curse in this place we'd be dead fifty times over.

"Peter and I went back to the Guard Room about 7.30 am, had some coffee and did two more rounds of the museum before the new shift came on. Never having seen that chap Mason, I examined his papers which seemed to be in order. John—that's John Mackay—noticed the control key was missing, but Peter gave it to him, and we left.

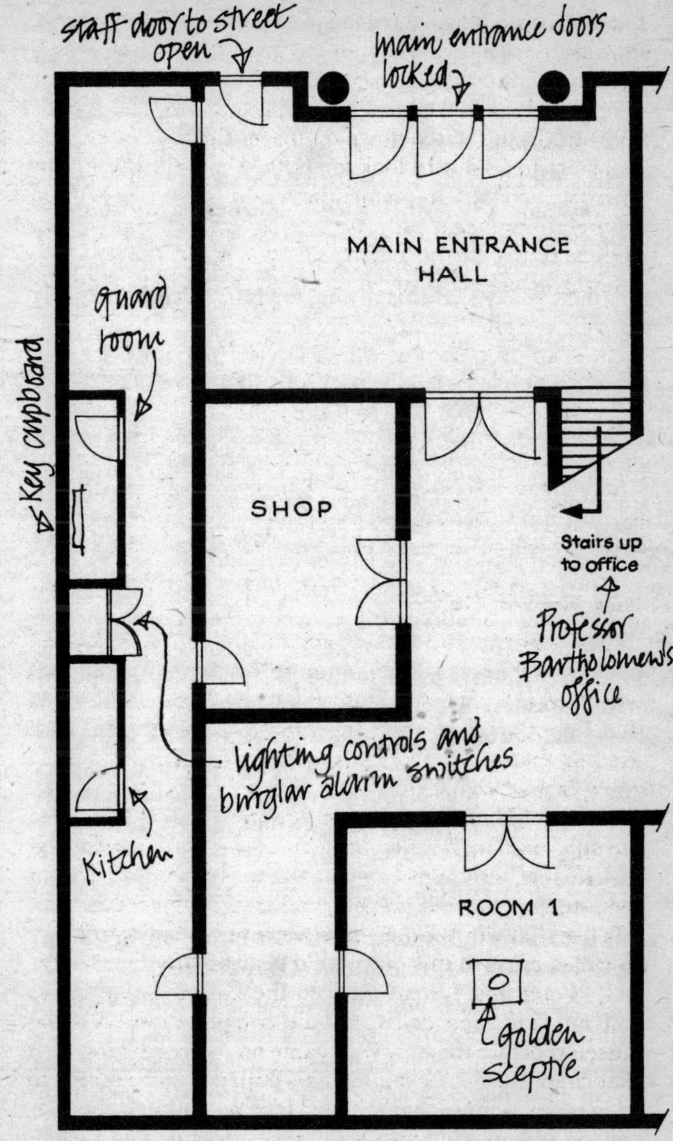

A plan of the museum showing the Superintendent's notes.

The next thing I knew I was being wakened and asked to come back because of the robbery. I'm sorry, but that's all I know."

Peter Haskins, Guard

"It was Alex and me who watched the sceptre being put in the museum. I'd shut down the alarm system from the main power unit, but forgot to put it back on again, as I still had the key in my pocket for the cupboard. I'm very ashamed to say that this means the burglar alarm system was not working for about six hours.

"It's that part of it which worries me most. I know I'm retiring in a few months, but I still don't reckon that's any excuse to slip up. To tell the truth, I feel responsible for the whole thing. If only I'd been more careful. Mind you, I'm not trying to defend myself, but I think all this stuff lying around is sore temptation for any man. What surprises me is that we've had so blooming few robberies in this place all the years I've been here.

"Anyway, it was lucky that old John noticed the key was missing from that cabinet over there—the one beside the other row of keys. These keys, by the way, are for other doors in the museum, including the small door beside the main entrance. After I gave John the key, I carried on changing out of my uniform, went for a drink with Alex down the road at *The Goose and Hare,* and went home.

"I wasn't due on until two the next afternoon, so stayed up quite late, getting to bed about one in the morning. Then I'm wakened up and brought here for this statement."

Ahmid Kahmil, Special Representative of the Egyptian Government, Antiquities Department

"Of course it does not surprise me that the sceptre of Akmenon has disappeared. Consider yourselves very lucky, that is all. The sceptre has the power of life and death, if not handled correctly and in the correct attitude of mind.

"I have never made any pretence of the fact that the

sceptre in particular should not have left Egypt. The arguments of Professor Bartholomew about it being important for research leave me cold. I am a man who knows there are greater things involved. You are seeing one of them now. The great god Horus was well known for his miracles. I would not be surprised if the Golden Rod is now on its way back to its rightful resting place in Egypt.

"Apart from not wishing the sceptre to leave my homeland I was also against it coming to this particular museum. Last month, when I was given a detailed tour of inspection, I said the security was not sufficient. But I was told I was being over-sensitive and not to worry. Ha! So who's right now?

"But you must realise, Superintendent, that the sceptre is not of any use to anyone who does know of its powers. In fact, I would go as far to say that in the wrong hands it is positively dangerous, for the reasons I have already stated. I agree that if it was melted down it would be worth a great deal of money, but the gods help anyone who dares try that!

"I left the museum yesterday in a bad frame of mind, as I think you put it. I felt I had been insulted by your Professor Bartholomew, because he had scorned my deeply-held beliefs. I went to the Egyptian Embassy, and then spent the night at the theatre with a friend. Around midnight I returned to my hotel, and I was asleep when the disappearance occurred.

"All I have to add is that I have already reported the matter to my superiors in Cairo, and I can assure you that if the sceptre is not recovered very soon—assuming it is not already back in Egypt—it will be a very long time before the British Government will be allowed to have any more of our treasures in their country.'"

Detective Superintendent Brownlee went over the above statements very carefully before calling all the main witnesses together. He then carefully questioned them again, this time in front of each other. The stories were basically the same as in their statements.

'Well,' he finally said, 'my initial suspicion was correct.'

He then made an arrest, and collected the sceptre.

Obviously somebody is not telling the truth. The clues are fairly slim and it would take a fine eye for detail to spot some of them. The answers in the back will clear things up.

PARTICLES OF DEATH

'Well? Have you sorted out who did it?'

Sir Thomas Rogers, chairman of Industrial Research Ltd, the giant government-linked atomic research company, looked up somewhat sternly at Peter Whitley, his security chief for the company.

Whitley shook his head. 'I'm afraid not, sir. But once Karl Stevens turns up—to use his pseudonym—then we might get a few more answers.'

'Well, if what you say is true, he's probably back behind the Iron Curtain. But I really don't think his re-appearance will help. That's why I asked you to come here to-day.'

The men were sitting in Whitley's office at the laboratories in Kent, where research was carried out into uses of radiation.

'The trouble is, Peter,' Sir Thomas continued, 'the leaks are still taking place. Our people in Russia have informed us that scientists there are just beginning an experiment along the lines of Z750—which we only started ourselves two weeks ago! Someone is still passing information. So Bob Mason's death didn't stop *that*!'

'I don't know, sir' Whitley said. 'I mean, he was working on the bones of Z750 before he was killed.'

'Perhaps so,' the chairman conceded. 'But we won't know that until you come up with an answer as to who killed Mason. Now, exactly what have you got? You mentioned something about a report.'

'Yes, sir, I've got it here.' Whitley handed him a buff folder. 'But there's no answer in it. You used to work for intelligence during the war. You know how it's possible to kill someone and then disappear from sight with a great deal of information. I know I've spent nearly fifteen years working for a commercial security firm, and I've only been here three years, but I'm already realising that this business is open to all kinds of invisible threats to security.'

'That sounds like an excuse, Peter,' said Sir Thomas coldly. 'And you're not paid to make excuses after the event. It's your job to stop this sort of thing. I'll look at this report now and call you when I've finished.'

Whitley shrugged and left the office. Sir Thomas opened the folder in front of him. TOP SECURITY was written over the first page, followed by a short statement by Whitley saying he had prepared the report over three weeks, and then a list of the people he had interviewed for it.

There were four names on the list: Dr Graham Sedgewick, the Chief of Research on the project; Keith Burnham, another scientist working with Bob Mason; Penelope Miller, a laboratory assistant; and Karl Stevens, the cook. All four had been interviewed both at the scene of the death, Sir Thomas's country residence, and later in the labs.

After telling his secretary to hold all calls, Sir Thomas began to read the report.

Report on death of Dr R. Mason . . . . P. Whitley

I arrived at Towering Manor in the early evening of 26th May, 19—, having been asked down by Sir Thomas Rogers to discuss long term security plans in the light of the leak we had discovered. There was a message that Sir Thomas had been delayed in London until the following day. Sir Thomas's other guests were about to start dinner, so I joined them. Everyone seemed in good spirits and we stayed in the dining room talking and drinking until 10.30 pm. Feeling tired after my long journey, I went to my room at the top of the house and prepared for bed. My room was next to Bob Mason's and I heard him come up about half-an-hour later.

However, I could not sleep and lay reading. Around midnight I heard Mason's door open and close quietly and then his footsteps going along the corridor towards the hall. Curious, I followed. I reached the head of the stairs and looked down into the hall. I just glimpsed a shadowy figure disappearing off somewhere to the right, towards what I later found to be the kitchen. I presumed Mason was going for a nightcap, and returned to my room.

Two things then happened which caused me to dress quickly and leave my room for further investigation. First of all, I heard a quiet buzz, so I headed immediately for the back door near the kitchen. As I got to the head of the stairs again, I heard Mason shout 'No!' and then a thud (which was Mason falling). I rushed down the stairs, and as I did so, I heard a car starting up outside the main door. Running across the hall, I looked out of the side windows by the door and saw a car driving out of the front gate.

As there was a full moon I was able to catch sight of the number plate (BJA 254). As you know, this car was later found abandoned in a nearby town, and as you further know, it belonged to Karl Stevens.

However, as I was concerned about Bob Mason, I hurried to the kitchen. I found him there, lying on the floor dead. There was an odd, sharp smell in the vicinity.

As you know, there is an outhouse leading from the kitchen to the back garden, and a door in the outhouse which leads to the cellar. I noticed that the cellar door was slightly ajar, but thought nothing of it because the outside door was also open. I had just reached it when I was struck from behind and knocked out, falling behind the huge barrel which is kept in the outhouse.

I'm not sure how long I lay there, but I was wakened by the sound of the telephone ringing in the kitchen. I lay in the darkness, feeling groggy and heard Karl Stevens speaking. He said that Bob Mason was dead and that he would meet the caller outside the railway station in

Frickby at seven in the morning. Then he hung up. I staggered to my feet and Stevens seemed surprised to see me. He then told me *he* had been knocked out also and had just wakened in time to answer the phone. He said it was the new kitchen help, who was stranded at Carlisle because of train trouble and would not be arriving until seven the next morning. (As you know, a new member of staff did arrive the next day.)

I phoned the local doctor. He diagnosed a heart attack. But it was discovered later at the autopsy that death had been induced by prussic acid, which is a favourite method of the KGB. (The system is straightforward. A glass phial is placed in a narrow tube about eight inches long. A spring in the tube sets off a small charge which crushes the phial, spraying the poison out as a vapour. When the acid is inhaled, the blood vessels contract, as in a normal heart attack. Once the victim is dead, the blood vessels relax and any examination of the body shows a cardiac arrest. Only in later post mortems is it possible to detect the acid.) *Mason had been murdered.*

I questioned the cook that evening, but he stuck to his story that he had heard a noise in the outhouse while he was clearing up in the kitchen and when he went to investigate, he was knocked out. I could not question him further, for as you are aware, he disappeared the next morning. I sent you a report on Karl Stevens, which shows he had contacts with the Russian Secret Service seven years ago, which he reported to British Intelligence, who checked him out. It is my belief that Stevens (who was in charge of catering at the labs) was still working for the KGB, and that he was going through your papers and those of the research team. Until we find him, of course, we will not be able to prove this.

The following are shortened versions of the interviews I held with the other guests in Towering Manor that night.

Statement by Dr Graham Sedgewick, Chief of Research

I went to my room about eleven o'clock. I accompanied Bob Mason up the stairs and wished him good-night. Having some papers to read, I sat up for a while after having a bath and changing into my pyjamas. Around midnight I heard some noises from the hall and a shout. Putting on my dressing gown, I rushed along the corridor and down the stairs.

As I reached the foot of the stairs, Penelope Miller came rushing out of the kitchen in a distressed state. She told me she had found Bob Mason lying in the kitchen. I had to return for my slippers first, as the stone floor in the hall was freezing cold. Miss Miller came with me and we knocked on the door of Mr Whitley's room, but there was no answer. On our return to the kitchen we found the cook, Mr Stevens, rubbing his head and complaining he had been knocked out. Miss Miller and I left him in the kitchen while we went to try and find Mr Whitley. The only other thing I noticed was that the red bulb outside the cellar, which tells if the light is on inside the cellar, was glowing. The door was open, so I peeped in—just inside there was a bottle lying on its side, which I presumed had been used to knock out poor Mr Stevens. I wandered about the house looking for Mr Whitley, but on my return to the kitchen found him there, saying that he too had been knocked out. That is all I can remember about that awful night.

[While reading the statements, Sir Thomas had been jotting down notes on a large pad by his side. As he did so, he sighed repeatedly. Bob Mason had been a close friend of his for many years, and he still couldn't accept the fact that he was dead. Sir Thomas felt particularly bad about his own absence on the night of the murder. Shaking his head slowly, he picked up the report again and began to read Penelope Miller's statement.]

Statement by Penelope Miller

After dinner and drinks, Keith Burnham and I went out

the front lawn to walk around the walled garden. It was a clear night and we were admiring the weeping willows and the marvellously shaped hedges. Being interested in old houses myself, and knowing Keith to have a similar interest, I got us talking about Towering Manor. We sat on one of the stone benches and chatted for about half-an-hour, wondering what the manor would have been like in the days of the Civil War, when priests were hidden in secret places in the building. Keith said he had visited Towering Manor a number of times before, and knew of some secret passages, one which ended not ten feet from us. He showed me what looked like a drinking well, but when he turned a small statue on it, it swung open. Excited, I followed him down the passage in the dark holding his hand. Eventually we started going up a slope and came out in the cellar of the house! Keith said he was going back to close the door at the other end and would see me in the kitchen. I was feeling thirsty anyway, so I went straight up there. That's when I found Bob lying on the floor and ran into the hall, met Dr Sedgewick and went looking for Mr Whitley.

When we got back to the kitchen the cook was there, holding his head. I went down into the cellar to find Keith but he wasn't there. The lights were on in the cellar and along the passage so I went through. But the garden door was closed. I went back to the kitchen, found Mr Whitley, and was up most of the night. That's all I know.

Statement by Keith Burnham

It seems as if I missed most of the action, I'm afraid. After dinner I went into the garden with Penelope for a walk. We must have strolled about for about half-an-hour and then we sat and chatted for about the same time. I was telling her about the secret passages in the old manor, and showed her one that led from the garden to the cellar. Penny went upstairs for a drink and I returned to close the garden entrance. As I was walking along the passage in the dark I heard a car start up and drive towards the main gate. I wondered who was driving around at that time of night—about midnight—and hurried up to the garden. I saw a black car driving away from the gate. Closing the secret passage door, I went back to the house. I saw someone in the outhouse, but before I could see who it was, he or she disappeared behind the huge barrel there. I tried to get into the outhouse, but the door was jammed, so I had to go round to the side entrance of the house, which was open.

I came along the back passage to the kitchen and found Mr Stevens on the phone. I heard him arranging some sort of meeting while I hid in the passage. I did this because I've heard so much about security, it's got that I can hardly trust my own shadow. As I stood there I saw Penelope rush into the kitchen and tell Karl Stevens Bob was dead. He said he knew and was going to phone the police. But he didn't as Mr Whitley suddenly appeared from the outhouse and began questioning Stevens. They both went into the library and I came out into the kitchen.

There was a bitter smell, and I saw Bob Mason lying at the side of the kitchen door. Beside him there was a piece of paper, which I stupidly picked up, not thinking about fingerprints. It was just some notes Bob had been making on Project Z750, nothing secret, but certainly of interest to anyone wanting to know what we were doing. As I was looking at the paper, I heard a movement behind me from the direction of the cellar. As the cellar door was just round the corner out of sight, I went to see who it was.

I reached the door as it was being closed, and I heard footsteps going down the steps. I tried to open the door, but there was a Yale lock on it and I couldn't open it. I went into the outhouse and looked in the garden, and saw the other entrance to the underground passage open, and Penelope Miller come out, looking a little frightened and confused. She ran across the garden, rang the bell, and I let her into the kitchen.

We answered a lot of questions for Mr Whitley and this recorded statement is the truth as far as I know it.

Burnham's statement, like the others, was signed. Whitley had added a conclusion, in which he stated his belief that the guilty party must have been the cook, Karl Stevens, and that the meeting Stevens was arranging was with one of the people he was working for—probably the Russians, judging from the cause of Mason's death.

Sir Thomas closed the folder containing the report and drummed his fingers lightly on top of it. Then he put a call through to Peter Whitley.

'Peter,' he said. 'You'd better get up here. I want you to be present when the police—whom I'm about to call—arrest the murderer of Bob Mason.'

There were a few moments of silence at the other end of the line.

'You mean it wasn't Karl Stevens?' Whitley asked in surprise. 'How did you work out who did it?'

'A question of intelligence, Peter,' Sir Thomas chuckled down the phone.

How's your IQ? Have you pinpointed the culprit?

NEPTUNE'S SECRET

Detective Inspector Jimmy Grant was not in the best of moods. Under normal circumstances he would have thoroughly enjoyed sitting in a deck chair on the deck of a luxury cabin cruiser, anchored off the Channel Islands. But he had been called out in the middle of a game of golf—when he was five strokes up. Apart from his work, Jimmy Grant took only one other thing seriously—his golf. So he sucked noisily and angrily on his pipe and gazed out at the sea, which sparkled under a flawless, blue sky.

'Sergeant Clark,' he said to the detective sergeant beside him. 'Stick close to me and listen well. I want this thing wrapped up quickly—if not, I'll leave it to you to finish.'

'Yes, I heard you were five up when you got the message,' the sergeant said, trying to hide a smile.

'Are you saying I put my pleasure before my work, boy?' Grant thundered at the 35-year-old 'boy'.

'Never, sir, never,' the other detective said seriously.

'Good,' Grant snapped. 'Well let's not waste any more time. You were here before me. Fill me in on the facts, please. And no theories, just facts,' he added and sucked at his empty pipe once more.

'I arrived here at nine-fifteen in answer to a radio call. Terence Granger lay dead in his diving suit over there, sir,' he said, pointing to a spot on the deck where a pair of compressed air tubes lay. 'It seems as if Mr Granger went diving around seven-thirty this morning. . .'

'Alone?'

'Yes, sir. A very foolish thing to do, I know.'

'Bloody dangerous thing to do,' Grant commented. 'Of course what do you expect with amateurs and fools. Go on, sergeant.'

'He'd been down about an hour when the captain noticed there were no bubbles coming up from the sea and then Mr Granger's body comes floating to the top, dead as a dodo.'

'Your descriptions could be a bit more subtle, sergeant,' Grant glared. 'Did you get a doctor out here?'

'Yes, sir. One came with me. He examined the body in a spare cabin and said Mr Granger had died of a heart attack and also lack of oxygen.'

'Is that all he said?' Grant asked irritably.

'No, sir,' Clark replied. 'He said that the heart attack could have been brought on by shock when Granger realised he did not have enough oxygen left in his tanks. You see, sir, the tanks were empty when the body floated to the top. These, sir, are the facts.'

'Not quite, sergeant,' Grant corrected him, taking his pipe out of his mouth. 'Who were the last people to see him alive, and what was he doing diving at the unearthly hour of seven-thirty?'

'His manservant, Robert Courcy, and his wife, Patricia, saw him—she's been put out for the count by the Doc. . .'

'We really must send you to English lessons,' Grant muttered. 'Who else?'

'Jonathan Bell, a friend and business partner of Granger's, and Bill Rafferty, the first mate. Oh, and the captain, Tom Morton said he saw him this morning briefly,' the detective added. 'But as to why they were here, I was about to find that out when you arrived, sir.'

'Good, well let's start talking to everyone concerned,' Grant said, looking at his watch. 'Time moves on. Ask the manservant to come here, would you?'

Despite the temperature, Courcy was dressed in a

three-piece black suit.

'So you're the butler, or manservant, or whatever they call you nowadays,' said Grant, as Courcy sat down in a lounge chair opposite him. 'You didn't do it, did you?' he smiled.

The expression, or lack of it, on Courcy's face showed Grant the joke had fallen flat.

'Okay, tell me what happened here this morning before Mr Granger went below.'

'He went diving, sir, and when he surfaced he was dead,' Courcy replied, stony-faced.

'Don't be funny with me, Mr Courcy,' Grant snapped, waving his pipe at the manservant. 'I want to know what Granger did from the time he woke to the time he went into the sea.'

'Very well, sir,' Courcy replied flatly. 'I woke Mr Granger at precisely 7 am as he had instructed. I gave him his usual cup of coffee, and he showered before changing into his diving suit which hung behind the cabin door. I remained in the cabin tidying his clothes.'

'Where was Mr Granger?'

'On the deck, of course, preparing to don his air tanks.'

'So the air tanks are kept up here?'

'Yes, sir,' Courcy replied. 'In the storage room over there,' he said, waving his hand behind him. 'Mr Rafferty is in charge of the tanks and always helped the divers prepare before they went down.'

'Did Mr Granger normally go down on his own?'

'Of course not, sir. Even I know that at these depths one should be accompanied by another diver in case of trouble. He normally dived with Mr Bell, one of his business partners.'

'Then doesn't it strike you as odd that he decided to go it alone this morning?'

'Not in the least, sir,' Courcy answered stiffly. 'When Mr Granger arranged to do something he did it. The fact Mr Bell was ill did not deter Mr Granger.'

'Yes, I'd heard of his reputaton,' Grant commented.

'Was he just going down for pleasure?'

'I hardly think we would choose to be stuck off the coast of Jersey for pleasure,' Courcy answered, ignoring the detective's look of fury. 'Mr Granger was looking for sunken treasure, having acquired a map which showed that a Spanish galleon, loaded with jewels and money, had sunk here in the eighteenth century.'

'Very interesting,' Grant muttered. 'I don't think the Government knows about this, or I would have heard about it. Did he find anything?'

'Yes, sir. Yesterday he brought up some stuff for the first time—a small rotted chest and a couple of doubloons. Mr Bell salvaged an old sword.'

'Hmmm,' Grant nodded. 'So the last time you saw Mr Granger was when he left the cabin to put his air tanks on. What sort of a mood was he in, would you say?'

'Not too good,' Courcy replied. 'You see, he hadn't been feeling too well when I woke him. And illness only irritated Mr Granger.'

'What was wrong with him?'

'He was complaining of stomach pains and pins and needles in his legs and arms,' Courcy said.

'Good God!' Grant exclaimed, sitting forward suddenly. 'Had he complained about this before?'

'Not to my knowledge, sir,' the manservant replied, looking surprised at Grant's outburst.

'Tell me, when did Mr Granger last have something to eat or drink before his coffee this morning?'

'Last night, I believe,' Courcy said. 'He usually had a cup of hot milk before retiring.'

'And did you give it to him last night?'

'No, sir. Normally Mrs Granger made it for him and took it to his cabin.'

'You mean Mr and Mrs Granger did not share the same cabin?' Grant asked incredulously.

'Not of late, sir,' the servant said quietly.

'Why's that?' Grant snapped. 'Come on, man, I want to know. Don't look so sheepish. We could be investigating a murder here!' he added, glancing at Sergeant Clark.

'Well. . .well. . .,' Courcy stammered. 'You see things had not been going well between Mr and Mrs Granger for some time. I thought it had reached a head this morning when I overheard. . .' he trailed off, and looked down, unsure of what to say.

'Heard what, man? Heard what?' Grant shouted.

'Well, I was in the cabin as I said, when this argument—or to be precise, I heard *two* arguments between Mr Granger and Mr Bell and then Mr and Mrs Granger.'

'How could you hear this from the cabin?'

'The porthole was open,' Courcy claimed. 'It would appear as if Mr Granger was angry at the attentions Mr Bell was giving to Mrs Granger. He told Mr Bell this morning to "lay off" his wife, "or else". He then reminded Mr Bell that if it had not been for Mr Granger, he would still be an accountant in a small office. Mr Bell burst out laughing and said it was too late for that kind of talk as he was now a partner and would probably be the next chairman. "Over my dead body," Mr Granger told him. Mr Bell laughed again and said, "If that's the way you want it, that's the way you'll get it," and walked off.'

'What about the row between Mr and Mrs Granger?'

'She came on deck not long after Mr Bell had gone, and told her husband that she was tired of "his philandering" ', Courcy said.

'What did she mean by that?'

'I would take it she was referring to the attentions he was paying to Miss Winters, his new personal secretary. Mrs Granger added she "had had enough" and "wanted a direct answer".'

'To what?' Grant inquired.

'I'm afraid I have no idea, sir,' Courcy said. 'She walked away just then and Mr Granger prepared to dive.'

'Thank you, Mr Courcy, you've been most helpful,' Grant said. 'I'll call you if I need you again.'

After Courcy had gone, Grant turned to Clark.

'Did you hear all that, lad?' he asked. 'Especially the bit about the stomach pains and the tingling in the arms and legs?'

'I did, sir, I did,' the sergeant nodded.

'You know what that means, I presume?'

'No, sir,' Clark shook his head.

'My God, what *do* they teach at police college nowadays?' he asked raising his eyebrows. 'These are the symptoms of arsenic poisoning!'

'Good Heavens, of course!'

'I think we'll take a stroll down to Mr Granger's cabin and see if the cup which held his milk is still there,' Grant suggested and stood up.

The master cabin was spotless. Wall to wall cupboards ran along one side and a large bed filled most of the space. There were two portholes opposite the door, one of which was open. Grant walked across and gazed out of the open porthole.

'Calm sea,' he muttered, watching the waters of the English Channel bobbing gently.

Just then there was a crash followed by the sound of chains immediately above them, and shouting.

'I suppose that's known as dropping the anchor,' Grant chuckled. He looked around. 'It would appear as if the cup had been removed,' he said. 'You've checked the bathroom, I suppose?'

Clark nodded and then followed Grant back on deck. The inspector told Grant to find Jonathan Bell and bring him above.

Jonathan Bell, in his thirties, was about ten years younger than Granger. He was wearing a blue blazer and flannels, and was handsome in a classic way.

'I'll not waste time, Mr Bell,' Grant said after they had settled down in the deck chairs. 'I'd like to know about the row you and Mr Granger had this morning.'

'It was a ridiculous argument,' Bell sighed. 'And in the light of what happened I wish I'd kept my mouth shut. It started when I met Pat—Patricia Granger—on deck this morning at about quarter past seven. . .'

'Where exactly on the deck?'

'Near the storage cupboard where the diving gear is

kept. I was going to check my equipment,' Bell answered. 'Pat was in tears and told me she'd just had an argument with Terry—Terence Granger, that is—and had threatened to leave him if he did not stop employing Lesley Winters, his personal secretary. You see, Terry and Lesley were. . .'

'I know, I've heard,' Grant interrupted. 'What did you do after Mrs Granger had told you this?'

'I went and saw Terry myself to try and smooth things over between him and Pat. But he turned on me and accused me of all sorts of things. I saw it was useless to argue further, so left.'

'Why didn't you dive with him this morning, Mr Bell?' Grant asked, changing his line of questioning.

'I didn't feel too well—a touch of the hangovers,' he added, grinning weakly.

'And you had no intention of going into the sea, then?'

'I couldn't have faced it, I'm afraid, especially after that awful sudden storm last night,' Bell said. 'We were going pretty deep.'

'And what did you do after your row?' Grant asked.

'I went along to the stern of the boat and helped Rafferty with the tanks. Terry dived without saying anything more to me. I stood watching the bubbles for a while and then returned to my cabin to wait.'

'Wait? What for?'

'For. . . for Terry to come back up, of course,' Bell stuttered. 'When I thought I could perhaps make up our argument.'

'Did you actually help Mr Granger on with his tanks?'

'Yes, I held them while he slipped into them,' Bell replied.

'One final thing for the moment, Mr Bell,' Grant said. 'What is the nature of the e. . .em relationship between yourself and Patricia Granger?'

'We're close freinds, that's all,' Bell answered, his face flushing. 'I don't know what rumours you've been listening to, but I can assure you they're not true.'

'I haven't heard anything, Mr Bell,' the inspector told him. 'I have more important things to do with my time than listen to gossip,' he added, thinking of a particular golf-course not many miles from where they were sitting. 'I'll let you know if I need you again, Mr Bell,' he said, nodding at the sergeant, who rose and accompanied Bell to the head of the stairs leading down to the cabins.

'Who now, sir?' he asked, turning.

'Is Mrs Granger up to talking?' Grant asked.

'I think so, sir,' Clark replied. 'I saw her not so long ago. She seemed fine.'

'I'm not surprised,' the inspector mumbled. 'Okay, ask her to spare a few moments, would you?' he said aloud.

Patricia Granger had been a beautiful woman, and now in her forties she still retained a graciousness about her. Grant watched her sit opposite him, and realised why Terence Granger had called his cabin cruiser *Dark Beauty* in honour of her.

'I'm sorry to trouble you at a time like this,' he began. 'But I have to ask you a few questions.'

'I understand, inspector,' she said in a deep, husky voice. 'As you can see I'm not exactly shattered by the news.'

Even Grant, after twenty years in the force, was surprised by her coolness.

'Terry and I were hardly the picture of perfect matrimonial bliss over the past few years,' she went on. 'I won't bore you with the details, but it had reached the point where my life was becoming hell.'

'I know,' Grant said. 'But I'm interested in what happened here this morning—and last night. You took your husband some milk before he went to sleep didn't you?'

'Yes, but what's that got to do with this morning's accident?'

'Did you make the milk yourself?'

'Yes, I usually did,' she replied.

Grant looked quickly at Clark before continuing.

'And this morning, you had an argument. Why?'

'Over some personal matters. In fact I threatened to leave Terry unless he stopped seeing another woman.'

'So when did you last see your husband?'

'I think it was about quarter past seven,' she answered. 'I left him in a rage. I bumped into Jonathan on the deck and burst into tears and told him about my argument.'

'Where exactly did you meet Mr Bell?'

'Just outside the locker where the diving equipment is kept.'

'That's fine for now, Mrs Granger,' Grant smiled.

'Is that all?' she said in surprise.

'I said for now, Mrs Granger. I would like to run some tests on your husband's body.'

'Tests? What tests? He was killed in an accident,' Mrs Granger protested. 'Anyone can see that. It was an accident.'

'I wonder, I wonder,' the inspector said laconically.

Grant then asked to see Bill Rafferty, the first mate. Rafferty was a six-foot Irishman, broad and strong. He told Grant he had been a Merchant Seaman before going into the pleasure-cruising business about ten years ago. He added that it was his ambition to own a small fleet of pleasure cruisers of his own.

'That'll cost you a pretty penny, Mr Rafferty,' Grant smiled.

'Aye, sir. That's the only thing stopping me.'

'What do you know about this morning's events?' the inspector asked.

'I came up on deck about twenty past seven to help Mr Granger with his gear. I went to the storage locker to get the tanks. I was surprised to find the door open, as it was normally locked. . .'

'Who has the keys, Mr Rafferty?'

'Myself, Mr Granger and Mrs Granger had a spare set,' he replied. 'Well, as I say, the door was open, and I met Mr Bell coming out of the locker. He said he was checking his gear, but then said he'd decided not to go down. I said I knew how he felt, and went into the locker. It was a right mix-up, sir,' the first mate said. 'You know that terrible squall we had in the middle of the night? Well, it had knocked all the tanks and stuff off of the shelves and there was gear all over the place. I sorted some tanks out and took them up to Mr Granger.'

'When was the last time you checked the tanks?'

'Two days ago, sir,' Rafferty replied.

'But there was a dive yesterday. 'Didn't you fill them after that?'

'I. . . I. . . meant to, sir,' Rafferty claimed. 'But I had some shore leave and was keen to get off the boat and was going to fill them today.'

'How do you think Mr Granger died?' Grant asked suddenly.

'The way I see it is that he didn't have a full tank when he went down. Judging from the time he surfaced, he'd be on the seabed about twenty-five minutes when he realised. Normally two tanks give an hour and a half,' Rafferty explained. 'But it takes about twenty minutes to reach a depth of 100 feet—you've got to take it slowly to get used to the pressure, you see,' he added. 'Now, if he was at his full depth with empty tanks he'd have no chance. So, he tried to get up as quickly as possible. He probably panicked, poor blighter, like most amateurs. He'd try to kick his way up to the top, have no time to decompress properly, get a heart attack and float up.'

Grant said nothing for a few seconds. Then looking directly at the first mate said, 'When did you go down?'

'How. . . how. . . did you know?'

'Your hair's damp. And I presume you haven't just been washing it. Because if you had, you would have probably shaved—and it looks like you haven't done that today.'

Clark looked in open admiration at his superior.

'I went down just before lunch,' Rafferty admitted, 'to see if I could find anything to help the police.'

'You wouldn't have been looking for Spanish gold, by any chance? A small box of sparklers could buy a pretty fleet of boats, I would imagine.'

'What are you saying? I said I was trying to help. I haven't shaved because I didn't have time. I had a bit too much grog last night and stayed on shore all night with a mate of mine and didn't get back here until seven. I would have come back out, but for that storm.'

'Convenient. One thing, Mr Rafferty. Can't you tell if a tank is full or empty?'

'Afraid not. A full tank weighs roughly the same as an empty one. And, of course, the pressure remains the same whether a tank is a quarter full or completely topped up.'

'Of course,' Grant nodded. 'The tanks are filled with compressed air, so the pressure stays the same. Hmm. Finally, does each diver have his own set of tanks?'

'No, sir. We have about a dozen sets of the same make on board. We just take whichever one is ready,' the first mate answered.

'Well you've given me food for thought, Mr Rafferty,' the inspector smiled. 'Now I'm going to digest it. You can go now, and thank you for your time.'

Sergeant Clark leaned against the deck rail and watched Grant slowly fill his pipe, something he did to help him think. He then lit it, puffed for a few minutes and glanced at his watch.

'I think I might be able to get at least another nine holes in before the light gets too bad,' he commented. . .

'You know who did it, sir?' the sergeant asked in awe.

'Aye, lad, you could say that,' Grant smiled. 'Just me and old Neptune.'

Well, do you share the secret? You may be surprised with Grant's conclusion in the back pages, but there again you may not be!

SMASH HIT

The Presidents were one of the wealthiest pop groups in the country. Their fame was backed up by millions of sales—and not just to teenagers—both in Britain and abroad. So when their lead guitarist, Don Shelley, decided to quit the group to lead what he called 'a quiet life in the country', every newspaper columnist remotely connected with music began to talk about the 'tragedy for Britain' if the whole group split up. Even sober financial columnists spoke about the 'loss of earnings to this country'.

Their fears were groundless. the founder and leader of the group, Chuck Watson, announced that the guitarist would be replaced in the near future. What he did not announce was that he had been inundated with requests from other guitarists, some from high-powered groups, to join the band.

Chuck Watson was a mild-mannered, quiet-spoken young man of 28, who took his music very seriously. Unlike many pop musicians, he did not indulge in some of the more bizarre aspects of the business, and always took his wife and young baby son on tour with him. He was well-liked, and many said he brought out the 'mothering instinct' in older fans of the group. As one music paper put it, 'Chuck is the sort of boy every mother would like her daughter to go out with.'

He had announced that two guitarists were in the running for Shelley's place, and that he would not announce their names for obvious reasons. 'If their own bands found out, then the one who didn't get the job would be in trouble,' he explained at a press conference.

In fact, the guitarists were Bobby Slick of Bad Head and Don Preston of Rain, both well-known groups, but not in the same league as The Presidents. Slick and Preston were equally keen to have the job. As Slick put it to Chuck when he went along for an initial audition, 'It would be like becoming one of the Beatles.'

By the day of the next concert—scheduled to take place at Hammersmith, London—Chuck Watson had still not made up his mind. Even when the acoustics were being tested in the afternoon, he was still trying to decide.

Both Slick and Preston had been at the concert hall all day, under strict instructions not to show themselves because of the press. Both had separate dressing rooms in which they stayed most of the time.

What was worrying Chuck was the fact that both men were excellent guitarists in their own right, but he knew that anyone joining a band like The Presidents, which had been together for over ten years, had to have the right temperament. In other words, the final decision had to be based not only on playing skill, but personal judgement.

One hour before the concert was due to start, Chuck finally made up his mind. He went to Slick's dressing room and told the musician he had chosen him to play in the concert that night, which implied he would then join the group.

As he left the dressing room and was walking along the corridor a figure came running towards him, banged into him, and then roughly pushed him aside.

'What the. . .' he started. 'Why, John! What are you doing here?' he asked, as he recognised John Barrett, the Manager of Slick's group Bad Head.

'Don't try and soft-soap me, Chuck,' Barrett snarled. 'I've just found out you're trying to pinch Bobby Slick from us. Well, you won't get away with it! We need him for the next tour. Without him our group's finished.'

'But, John, you can have him for the tour,' Chuck said.

'So you say! I don't believe it,' Barrett snapped angrily. 'He's not going to play for you and that's the end of the matter!' he said and stomped off towards Slick's dressing room.

Chuck gazed after him for a few moments, shrugged and smiled wanly at two stage hands who had been watching in amazement, and then walked on down the corridor towards Don Preston's room to break the bad news to him. Preston was sitting in an easy chair, his feet propped up on his locked guitar case, reading a book when Chuck entered.

'Hi, Don,' Chuck said. 'I'll get straight to the point. We've decided to try Bobby Slick out.'

'Terrific,' Preston said flatly, not moving. 'My manager knows about me chasing the job. Now that I've lost out there's going to be some nice tension when I get back.'

'I'm sorry, Don,' Chuck sighed. 'I've just run into John Barrett, Slick's manager, and he's not too happy either. But you know what it's like in this business. It's just that Bobby's been playing longer than you have. He knows the wrinkles about settling in with another group. Okay?'

'Yeah, I suppose so,' Preston managed to smile. He stood and put his book on top of an amplifier. 'But I'm bloody annoyed!' he suddenly snapped and kicked the side of a loudspeaker beside the easy chair. 'I was really looking forward to playing with you.'

'I know, Don, I know,' Chuck muttered. 'Are you staying for the concert?'

'Might as well,' Preston said sullenly. 'Nothing else to do.'

'Come round later for drinks, all right?'

The guitarist nodded and smiled wryly. *'C'est la vie.'*

By the time Chuck had gone back to his own dressing room, changed, and tuned up his guitar there were only ten minutes left before the start of the concert. They had been told to meet in the side-wings just before going on stage. With five minutes to go, Bobby Slick had still not appeared.

'I'll go and see what the trouble is,' Chuck said, and set off for the dressing rooms. The corridor leading to Slick's room was empty as he walked along it. He knocked on the door.

'Bobby? You'll have to move it, baby,' Chuck called. 'We're on in a few minutes.'

There was no answer, so Chuck tried the handle. It turned easily and he pushed the door open.

'What are you. . .' he began to say, but the words dried up as he stared horror-struck into the room.

Bobby Slick lay face down in the centre of the floor, a knife in his back and a spreading pool of blood around him. . .

Inspector Billy Trent looked at the disconsolate musicians in front of him. They were sitting in the manager's office of the concert theatre. The concert had gone ahead as planned, with one exception. Don Preston had played in place of Bobby Slick. Trent had been called immediately, although by the time he arrived at the theatre, the concert was in progress.

'I told the lads the best thing to do was play,' the manager told Trent. He was a smooth-looking character with a shiny mohair suit. 'You know the old saying about the show going on.'

They were standing in the side wings, and Trent had difficulty in hearing the manager over the blare of the mountain of loudspeakers only fifteen feet away from him. He indicated that they should move away from the din.

'Much as I appreciate modern music,' the inspector said, 'I'm afraid the finer points are lost on me. Do you think I can use your office?'

'Of course, of course,' the manager said.

As they walked through the back wings of the building, two ambulancemen passed them carrying a stretcher with the covered body of Bobby Slick. There were police fingerprint experts and uniformed constables all over the place, watched by mystified stage hands.

Trent had waited in the manager's office, while the

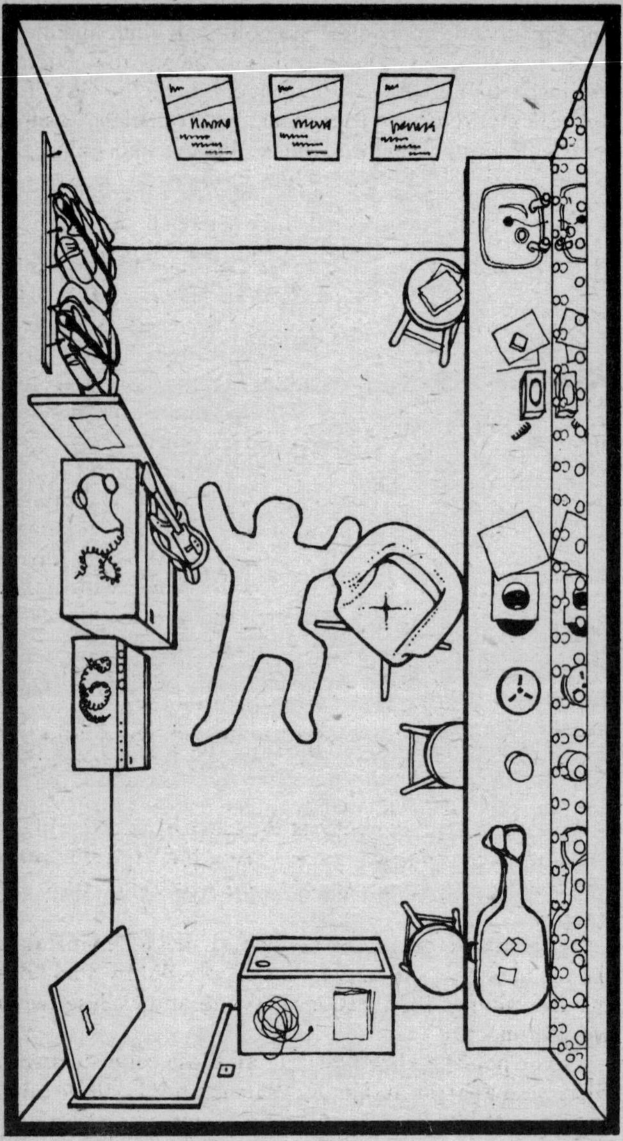

various detectives reported to him. They had found no fingerprints on the murder weapon, a six-inch flick knife which was brought along in a polythene bag to the detective inspector and now lay in front of him on the desk. The police doctor reckoned the killing had taken place no more than half-an-hour before Chuck Watson had found the body. There were no other clues in the dressing room as far as could be seen.

About fifteen minutes before the concert was due to end, Trent had gone along to the dressing room in which Slick's body had been found. Fingerprint experts were still dusting the room, and a photographer was taking some final shots for the files. A chalked outline on the floor showed where the body had lain. Trent glanced around the room. Various pieces of electronic equipment—amplifiers, loudspeakers and echo chambers—were piled against one wall; a guitar lay at an angle against them. A small partition jutted out about two thirds way down the wall, and behind it two suits of clothes hung on hangers from hooks on the wall. Down the opposite wall a mirror ran from one end of the room to the other, with naked bulbs around it. A long counter ran the length of the mirror, and a few stools were tucked under it.

Trent was looking around the room when a uniformed sergeant interrupted his thoughts.

'Excuse me, sir,' the policeman said. 'We found this down the corridor and I thought it may be of interest,' he added, handing Trent a glove.

The sergeant was holding the glove by the edge of the cuff and Trent carefully took it from him. On the index and middle fingers smears of blood were reflected in the light.

'Thanks sergeant,' he nodded. 'Unless I'm mistaken the blood on this will match that of poor Bobby Slick. But in a few minutes I'll question everyone, and we'll see what we can uncover. . .'

The police had rounded up all those connected with Slick, and apart from Chuck Watson and the three other members of The Presidents—a drummer, a bass guitarist, and a vocalist—Don Preston, John Barrett and the manager of the theatre now sat before the inspector. The two stage hands who had witnessed the argument between Barrett and Chuck were also present.

'I've called you all here together to save time, although we'll be taking individual statements later,' Trent began. 'Perhaps you can tell me what you know, Mr Watson,' he asked, smiling, and doodling on the corner of a large pad in front of him.

'Well, it's awful,' Chuck sighed, obviously affected by the death. He then told Trent about his difficulty in deciding who to choose, about how he had finally reached his decision, and about his meetings with Slick and Preston. He also mentioned the argument with John Barrett.

As Chuck spoke, the detective jotted notes on his pad.

'What did you do after finding the body?' he asked, looking up.

'I rushed back into the corridor,' Chuck said. 'I saw Mr Pease, the manager, talking with John Barrett up at the far end, near the stage, and I told them what I'd found. We came in here to the office and Mr Pease talked me into going on with the gig after I'd mentioned Don Preston was still around. I suppose he was right—all these people in the audience expecting something for their money.'

'You then told Don Preston, I presume?' the inspector queried.

'No, not immediately,' Chuck replied. 'I went to his dressing room, hoping he would still be there. He was, but I reckoned if I told him Bobby was dead it would upset him too much. I simply told him that he would be playing that night despite what I'd said to him before.'

'What was his reaction?'

'He was surprised. Said he couldn't believe it, and hoped he would be able to fit in.'

'How would he know what tunes you would be playing?' Trent asked, a curious expression on his face.

'That's easy,' Chuck answered. 'Last week we spent a day each with Don and Bobby rehearsing. So there was no problem there.'

'Thanks. The question wasn't really relevant, but I was just curious,' Trent commented. 'To go back to just before the concert again. You and Don Preston joined the others, I suppose.'

'Yes, that's it,' Chuck said. 'We were due on in a few minutes, at nine o'clock. Don was wearing jeans and an open-necked shirt and asked if he was dressed okay. Normally we dress the same in the band, but the way I was feeling I told him just to come along as he was. So he picked up his guitar and we joined the other guys backstage. As you know, the concert was a success.'

'So when did you tell Don about Bobby?' Trent wanted to know.

'About ten minutes ago, after the concert.'

Trent nodded, drew a line across the pad, and wrote down the name of John Barrett.

'Mr Barrett, I know how you're feeling, so I won't ask you many questions,' he said. 'When was the last time you saw Bobby alive?'

'About twenty to nine,' Barrett answered. 'I know because after I left him I glanced at the big electric clock behind the stage.'

'What did you say to him when you last saw him?'

'I tried to talk him out of going with The Presidents,' Barrett replied, his voice flat. 'But it was useless. To be honest, we had a bit of an argument. I spent about five minutes trying to persuade him, but as I say it was hopeless. I threatened to sue him.'

'Did he appear troubled by this?'

'The very opposite,' Barrett said. 'I've known Bobby for years and he's never treated me the way he did tonight. He was cool, arrogant and told me to do what I liked, he didn't care any more. He was tuning his guitar at the time and almost ignored me as I spoke. I felt like a piece of furniture standing there at the door. But for all that,' Barrett sighed, 'I wouldn't wish him dead. He was one of the good guys in this business.'

Trent grunted. He reached down to the floor and picked up a clear polythene bag containing the blood-smeared glove.

'Do you recognise this, Mr Barrett?' he asked, holding the glove up.

'Why . . . yes. It's . . . it's mine,' Barrett spluttered. 'I lost it earlier on. Where did you find it?'

'Outside Bobby Slick's dressing room,' Trent said simply, and put the glove on the desk beside the knife.

The detective then questioned the other members of the group, but only one of them, Pete Nichols the drummer, had seen Bobby that night.

'I popped in to wish him luck for the gig,' Nichols said. 'That was just before I changed—between quarter past and half past eight, I reckon.'

'Were you friendly with him, then?'

The drummer hesitated.

'You'd better tell him, Pete,' Chuck interrupted. 'It's best if you do.'

Nichols nodded and breathed in deeply.

'When Chuck told me who was going to play, I wasn't too happy,' he said. 'The thing is that I'd worked with Don Preston before, a long time ago. We got on well and I reckoned he would be good for the band, even though he wasn't as experienced as Bobby with big-name bands. But it was Chuck's decision, and we had to go along with it.'

'Let me get this straight, Mr Nichols,' the detecitve said. 'You would have preferred Don Preston.'

Nichols nodded.

'And that's exactly what happened,' Trent commented. 'Was Bobby aware of your feelings?'

'I'm afraid so,' Nichols answered. 'After I wished him luck, he said he was sorry that my old mate wouldn't be joining me. I told him not to be so silly, but he began shouting at me, accusing me of trying to swing Chuck's decision. I yelled back at him not to be so blinking idiotic and later when he wasn't so excited he would see I only cared for the good of the band. And then I left him.'

'What time would this be?'

'Probably around half-past-eight.'

Trent next questioned the two stage hands who had witnessed the argument between Slick's manager and Chuck. They confirmed what Chuck had already said, so the inspector went on to question the manager of the theatre. Richard Pease.

'You were talking to Mr Barrett when Chuck broke the news to you. What had you been doing before?' he asked.

'Oh, just wandering around, checking everything was in order. The usual thing before a concert—seeing the band was happy, the lights in order and so on.'

'Had you seen Bobby?'

'No, but I passed his dressing room a few times between eight and nine,' the manager replied.

'And did you notice anything unusual?'

'Yes. Twice I heard raised voices from the room, and then I met John Barrett coming out looking angry and holding his gloves in his hands. I asked him if he was leaving and he said yes, because he couldn't stomach seeing Bobby play with another group. I told him to give the lad a break and at least be decent about Bobby. We walked along the corridor, and I asked him to stay at least for fifteen minutes until the band started playing. He stuffed his gloves in his coat pocket, I think, and I was calming him down when Chuck told us the news. I can't think of anything else,' he concluded.

'Thank you, Mr Pease, that's fine,' said Trent. 'Don, do you think you're up to answering a couple of questions?'

The guitarist nodded.

'Good. When did you last see Bobby?'

'About quarter to nine, I think,' Preston replied. 'I'd left my dressing room and was going to the bar for a drink before the gig started. I noticed the time on the big clock and remember thinking I still had time for a pint. I thought I should make the gesture to Bobby and wish him all the best with The Presidents. I was in the dressing room when John Barrett knocked on the door and yelled to be let in. Bobby looked worried and whispered for me to hide behind the partition where his clothes were and to listen to what happened. He said he wanted a witness in case Barrett started getting heavy. You see, I knew he and Barrett never saw eye to eye and Bobby had been trying to get rid of him for a while. As I went behind the partition Bobby said Barrett would probably take him to court and it would be better if there was a witness.'

'And what did you hear?' the detective asked.

'More or less what Mr Barrett's told you,' Preston said. 'All about suing, and something about making sure Bobby wouldn't benefit from his new job. Bobby didn't seem too worried and John left. I came out, wished Bobby luck and went back to my dressing room for my wallet which I suddenly remembered I'd forgotten. I was just leaving for the bar when Chuck came in and told me I was playing. And that's it from me, inspector.'

'I think that's all for now, gentlemen,' Trent muttered. 'Thank you for being so helpful,' he went on, looking at the notes he'd made. 'Now if you'll just wait for a few moments, I'd like to run over these points I've jotted down.'

There was silence in the office as the detective ran through the pages. Finally he leaned forward, picked up the knife and then the glove. Laying them down, he rubbed his chin and glanced across at the sergeant who was standing by the side of the door.

'Sergeant,' he said quietly. 'I want you to make an arrest. The charge is murder, and all I can say at this stage is that whoever did it is in for a long stretch of peace and quiet away from the hubbub of pop music.'

Trent then named the suspect.

Can you name the suspect? The answer section will provide you with the clues you should have seen.

A BLAST OF DEATH

The body of Sir Edward Newby still lay covered with a tartan rug in the shooting lodge when Inspector 'Jock' Wilson arrived just before midday on Sunday.

'How long's he been here?' the inspector asked the local sergeant who had called him.

'Since after the accident, sir—he was brought in about quarter to eleven,' the policeman replied.

The inspector walked across to the table and lifted the left-hand corner of the rug. From where he stood, Wilson found it difficult to believe Sir Edward was dead. The fair hair, swept back, and the strong features of the face, with its square, prominent jaw and the thin moustache, gave Newby the appearance of a sleeper. But when the inspector moved round to the right the illusion ended. The right side of Newby's head had been blown off, and what had been the baronet's hand was now a loose-hanging mass of bone and bloody flesh.

Jock winced almost imperceptibly before covering the body again.

'Give me the facts, sergeant,' he sighed, sitting in an antique oak chair. 'And then I'll start interviewing witnesses.'

Sergeant Stonelee, a large, pleasant-looking man, pulled out a small notebook from his top pocket and leafed through it.

'Sir Edward Newby was having one of his weekly pheasant shoots,' he began. 'It was scheduled to start at

10.00 am, the party leaving from the lodge where they all met beforehand for a drink of punch. But Sir Edward was late in arriving, and they didn't set off until about 10.15. They were down at the Greenback Woods, about fifteen minutes away, when the beaters scared some pheasant and the hunters took aim.' The sergeant paused and glanced at the inspector, who sat with hooded eyes concentrating on what the policeman was saying. 'There was an almighty bang and the gun Sir Edward was holding exploded in his hands, killing him instantly,' concluded the sergeant, putting his notebook away.

'Who was in the shooting party?' Wilson asked, remaining perfectly still, his eyes almost closed.

The sergeant puffed his chest out importantly and could not conceal a smile of satisfaction as he reached into another pocket in his tunic, pulled out a sheet of paper and offered it to the inspector.

'I thought you might ask that, sir,' he said. 'I've made up two lists. The one on the right hand side of the sheet is the hunting party and the other is those who stayed at the lodge.'

Wilson glanced at the list briefly.

'Well done, sergeant,' he said. 'I'll start with those out on the shoot. I presume you told everyone to stay?'

The policeman nodded. 'They're in the next room, sir,' he told Wilson, and started for the door.

'One thing, sergeant, before you bring them in,' Jock said. 'Why did you call me in? Didn't you think it was an accident?'

The country policeman hesitated before answering.

'I'm not sure, sir,' he replied. 'I've lived in this part of the world most of my life and you get a feeling for things, if you know what I mean. I knew Sir Edward and would call him an expert gunman. It just doesn't add up that he would load a gun wrongly.'

'What do you mean?'

'It's a classic accident, sir. I saw something similar years ago, when a gamekeeper lost most of his hand.'

Wilson shifted his position in the chair and stared at

the sergeant. 'So you know how it happened?'

'Yes, sir. Once your ballistic chap is finished with the gun, I'm sure he'll agree. It's all to do with the cartridges,' he explained. 'As you know a twelve-bore cartridge is larger than a twenty-bore. And that's how it happened.'

The inspector looked blankly at the policeman for a few moments, and then stood up.

'Sergeant,' he said quietly. 'Would you tell me what in heaven's name you're talking about?' he asked, his voice rising angrily.

For a brief moment the sergeant looked disdainfully at his superior, and then remembering that Wilson was a 'city man' he explained further.

'Well, I reckon there was a twenty-bore cartridge in the barrel when Sir Edward pressed the trigger of his twelve-bore gun. That would mean the larger cartridge would smash into the smaller, and they would both explode inside the barrel, with the results you see in front of you,' he added, nodding slightly at the body.

'Either I'm very stupid, or don't follow what you're saying, but how can you load two bullets into one chamber, sergeant?'

'Oh, I don't think you're stupid, sir,' Stonelee said with a straight face, but he quickly went on when he saw the look Wilson gave him. 'You see, at the end of a cartridge there's a rim which holds it at the end of the barrel in the chamber. So if you drop a twelve-bore cartridge into a twelve-bore gun it's held there until fired. But if you drop a twenty-bore—which is smaller, don't forget—into a twelve-bore, it falls through the chamber into the barrel. But the rim holds it inside the barrel. You can't even see it there when you load up with the right bullet. So there's no way of telling until the trigger is pressed.'

'Thank you, Sergeant Stonelee,' Wilson said calmly. 'I've got the picture now. You think someone deliberately put the smaller cartridge inside the gun knowing what would happen when it was fired?'

'Oh, I don't know about that, sir. But you can be sure

Sir Edward didn't do it himself. He was too experienced—he could tell the size of a cartridge just by holding it.'

'Is there another room here where I can interview?' asked the Inspector. 'Preferably with a table.'

The sergeant led him to a side room.

'Send in the members of the shooting party first, would you, please. One by one.'

Wilson saw the two neighbours of the late baronet first, Sir Percy Brown and Peter Smythe. Both men had arrived together shortly before ten, had had the traditional drink of punch in the shooting lodge, and then set off when Sir Edward arrived. Both claimed they noticed nothing peculiar or suspicious and were shocked at the accident.

'Did Sir Edward provide guns or did you bring your own?' he asked each man separately.

Both neighbours had brought their own guns but the question reminded Sir Percy of an incident on the shoot.

'Edward actually forgot his gun,' he told the inspector. 'Or rather, his gamekeeper, Charles Blackthorne, forgot it.'

'So what did he do?'

'John Thorne, his cousin, said he would return to the lodge for Sir Edward's gun, and gave him his own.'

'You mean Sir Edward was using John Thorne's gun when he was killed?'

Sir Percy nodded.

'Was Thorne around when the accident happened?'

'No, as I said he had gone to collect Sir Edward's gun.'

'Why didn't the gamekeeper go for it?'

'I don't know,' Sir Percy shrugged. 'John Thorne offered and the gamekeeper stayed with us for a few minutes.'

'You mean Blackthorne also left the shoot?'

'Yes, Blackthorne discovered they were low on cartidges, and said he'd better go back to the lodge too to replenish his stock.'

'So the gamekeeper wasn't around when Sir Edward died?' Wilson queried.

'No, he was returning to the lodge. Which left only Alexander and Robert Newby, myself and Peter Smythe as well as the beaters.'

The inspector was silent for a few seconds.

'That's fine for now, Sir Percy,' he said finally.

'One more thing—would you say Sir Edward was a good neighbour?'

'Perfect,' the baronet replied.

Alexander Newby was the next witness to be shown in by Sergeant Stonelee.

'I'm afraid I'll have to speak for my brother Robert as well for the moment. He's taking this very badly,' Newby said as he sat opposite the straight-faced detective.

'I understand,' Wilson commented. 'Were he and Sir Edward very close?'

'Not really. But Robert feels particularly bad because he had just had an argument with Edward. Oh, it was nothing very serious,' he added hastily, with a wave of his hand. 'Robert and I are junior partners in the family business. Edward wanted to invest a lot of money in a Middle East engineering contract and Robert was against putting up so much risk capital. But we're always arguing over things like that and inevitably they blow over.'

'Your brother Edward was an expert gunhandler, I gather?' Wilson asked. 'Did he always load his own gun?'

'Yes, he made a point of it,' Newby answered. 'But . . . now you mention it, he didn't load up before the accident. I remember now,' he added, looking puzzled. 'John Thorne had given him his gun saying it was already loaded. Edward cracked the barrel and checked the chamber, and then snapped it into position again.'

'This was just before the accident?'

'Oh, about five minutes before I would say. John went back to the lodge for Edward's gun.'

'Do you know why your brother was late in arriving at the lodge this morning?'

'Yes, but . . . but I don't think that's relevant,'

Newby said quickly.

'Let me decide what's relevant, please,' Wilson said with an icy smile.

Alexander Newby breathed in deeply.

'Very well, but I don't want this to be generally known,' he sighed. 'Lady Newby had gone ahead to the lodge about half-past-nine. I was pottering about getting changed in the mansion when I heard raised voices along the corridor from my bedroom. I looked out and saw Edward and Sir John Carson—one of the other house guests—shouting at each other. They were arguing about that Middle East contract I've already mentioned. John Carson, as you probably know, owns a rival engineering company but he and my brother have been friends for years,' he added, and then paused.

'So what's so secret about that?' Wilson demanded.

'Nothing. But it's what happened next that I don't want known. You see, John Carson said that unless my brother forgot about the contract he would expose the relationship between my brother and Carol Grayson, Edward's private secretary.'

Newby lowered his head in obvious embarrassment after telling the detective. Wilson gazed at him for a few seconds.

'Don't worry,' he said. 'I'm not going to spread it around. But tell me more about this contract which keeps cropping up.'

'Carson needed it because his company wasn't doing too well. From what I can gather he wanted Edward to help him for old times' sake by not tendering, in which case there was a very good chance Carson would walk away with it.'

'So why was Robert worried?'

'He thought the contract was a bad one. The sheikh we were dealing with has a bad reputation for not paying—and I must admit I wasn't too happy about the deal either.'

'Thank you,' Wilson nodded. 'Now tell me—did you and Robert take along your own guns?'

'Yes, we always did,' Newby answered. 'They're kept in a locked cabinet in the lodge.'

'And did you have enough cartridges for the shoot?'

'Yes. I loaded up before we left. And Charles Blackthorne always carried extra boxes, but he forgot this time and went back to get some.'

'That's all for now, thank you,' Wilson smiled. 'Oh, sorry, one thing more. Would you call Sir Edward a proficient gunhandler?'

Newby smiled. 'Well, he held the area championship in rifle shooting.'

'And yourself? Are you proficient?

'I would say so.'

'Thank you. Sergeant?' he asked, turning to Stonelee who stood in front of the door. 'Could you ask Mr Thorne if he could spare some time?'

The sergeant held the door open for Newby and then followed him out. A few moments later John Thorne entered. Thorne was a tall, gaunt man in his early forties. The inspector watched him slump into the chair.

'I don't know what all these questions are for,' Thorne suddenly said. 'We've had an accident and that's it.'

'So you're sure it was an accident?' Wilson snapped.

'You . . you're not saying it was deliberate, are you? Cartridges jam you know. People get killed every season with this sort of thing.'

'No doubt, Mr Thorne, no doubt,' Wilson said laconically. 'I merely want to know what happened, that's all. I'm not saying anything. Now, tell me, please, why did you decide to go back for Sir Edward's gun and give him your own?'

Thorne smiled thinly.

'I know what you're thinking, inspector. I fixed my gun and then handed it over to him knowing it would explode. Well, sorry. The answer's much more basic. I had a bit too much to drink last night and was feeling the effects. I gave my gun to Edward and hoped to go back to the lodge where I could sit in peace and quiet.'

'But you didn't go back, did you?'

'How do you know?'

'Inspired guess, Mr Thorne. What the detective books call a hunch.'

'Well, of course I didn't go back. I heard this huge bang a few minutes after I left the party, and rushed back to see what had happened. As a matter of fact, I helped carry Sir Edward to the lodge,' he stated. 'And I don't know if you realise it, inspector, but that could have been me lying in the next room had I fired the gun.'

'The thought had crossed my mind, Mr Thorne,' Wilson commented. 'But why would anyone want to kill you?'

'If you must know, plenty of people. For a start, Edward and I were not exactly kissing cousins. Years ago I started a business with money lent to me by Edward. The business flopped and I owed Edward a fortune, a fact he and his brothers constantly reminded me about it,' he said bitterly. 'Well, I approached Edward some months ago about a Middle East contract I could get together. . .'

'Oh, not again,' Wilson muttered.

Thorne looked puzzled but continued.

'Edward was all for it, but Robert was convinced I was up to something, and tried to talk Edward out of it. So Robert would have been pleased if I had been the one to pull that trigger.'

'Who else? You said you had plenty of enemies.'

'Perhaps I exaggerated,' Thorne said, trying to smile. 'But I know that my partner's not too happy with me trying to get Edward to back the Middle East venture.'

'And who's that?'

'Sir John Carson.'

The inspector showed no emotion at hearing this piece of news, but continued his questioning.

'If I could get back to the actual death, Mr Thorne,' he said. 'You were not present, I gather.'

'That's so,' Thorne nodded. 'As I said I was on my way to the lodge.'

'You knew your way to the lodge without guidance?'

Thorne laughed dryly.

'I spent every childhood holiday with my cousins,' he pointed out.

'And how far were you from the lodge when you decided to go back?' Wilson asked.

'Oh, about ten minutes I would estimate.'

'Yes, it all seems to fit,' the inspector muttered, and then louder, 'thank you for being so helpful. The sergeant will show you out. And sergeant, could you ask Mr Blackthorne, the gamekeeper, to come in?'

Charles Blackthorne was still wearing his boots and shooting jacket. A square, strong-looking man, he seemed the type that brooked no nonsense and spoke bluntly, an impression which was backed up from his first comment.

'It's no bloody accident, if you ask me, sir,' he said as he sat down. 'I've seen that kind of thing before. Double cartidges in the gun. A twenty-bore I'll be damned—down the barrel. It's an old trick.'

Wilson noticed Sergeant Stonelee smiling in the background.

'Yes, yes,' he sighed. 'So I've been told. You were not present when Sir Edward was killed. Why?'

'I was going back to the lodge for some cartridges,' the gamekeeper replied.

'Why were you short of cartidges in the first place?'

'It was one of these mornings. First of all, Sir Edward not turning up on time. Then me losing my keys for the gun cupboard . . .'

'You mean you couldn't get any guns out?' the inspector interrupted.

'No, it meant I couldn't lock the cabinet. It was one of Sir Edward's rules on account of his children, you see. The cabinet always had to be locked.'

'When did you realise you'd lost your keys?'

'That's the funny thing,' Blackthorne said. 'I got to the lodge about 9.30, let myself in, opened the cabinet and laid the keys down on the table at the door. I went to get them just before ten, when I think the Old Man . . .'

'You mean Sir Edward?'

'Yes,' the gamekeeper nodded, 'when I think Sir Edward is coming. The keys are not there. So we have a search for them, my wife and me—she's there to make the punch, you see—and then we find the keys eventually at the side of the gun cupboard. My wife says I probably put them on the narrow shelf in front of the cabinet and they fell down, but I can't remember doing that at all.'

'Then what happened?'

'Because I was running late—or so I thought— I unlocked the cabinet, let Alexander and Robert take their guns out and then John Thorne says he'd decided to go in spite of his thumping hangover and he takes a gun. I took my own gun down from the cabinet and just then Sir Edward appears with Sir John Carson and yells at us to get moving 'cause we're late and I forget the cartidges and that's why I've got to go back to the lodge in case they run out.'

Wilson nodded.

'You've been on plenty of these shoots before. Tell me what happens exactly.'

'The beaters go on ahead to scare the birds out of the undergrowth and the hunters follow close behind. When the birds fly up, the party aims and fires.'

'I'm sorry to appear so ignorant, but I am not a sporting man, Mr Blackthorne. What happens after the hunters have shot for the first time?'

'They reload, of course.'

'And Sir Edward, when did he load up?'

'Usually on the shoot, and would carry his gun at half-cock—that is, with the barrel hanging loose to put it in your kind of language.'

'I appreciate that. And also why you would need more cartridges,' the inspector smiled. 'And exactly when was it you started to go back to the lodge?'

'I'm not sure of the exact time, but I would say three or four minutes after Mr Thorne had set off,' the gamekeeper said.

'And then what happened?'

'I'm walking through the woods when I hear this

loud bang. I know it's not a normal gun sound, so rush back. The rest you know. Sir Edward was on the ground, the others round him. It was a nasty scene. We carried him back immediately, but as you know. . . he was. . . dead on arrival here.' The gamekeeper's voice faltered slightly as he spoke, and Wilson waited for a few moments before questioning him further.

'Who carried Sir Edward back, Mr Blackthorne?' he finally asked in a quiet voice.

'Let me see,' said the gamekeeper, trying to remember. 'There was myself, Robert Newby, Alexander and John Thorne. Sir Percy and Mr Smythe carried the gear and the beaters came along behind.'

'There's one other thing that puzzles me, Mr Blackthorne,' said Wilson. 'Why would a man like Sir Edward, an experienced hunter, go out on a shoot without his rifle?'

'I thought you might ask that,' the gamekeeper chuckled. 'I usually carried Sir Edward's gun up to the point of the actual shoot. And as I've already told you I'd had one of these mornings. Mind you, there was always a spare gun brought along, but the one I took Sir Edward was not fond of so he accepted John Thorne's gun. Sir Edward sometimes carried his own gun. But he seemed very upset this morning for some reason, and started off on the shoot as soon as he arrived.'

Inspector Wilson breathed in deeply.

'I think that's all for now. Sergeant Stonelee,' he said twisting round, 'ask Sir John Carson to step in, would you?'

The Inspector was standing by the window watching a darkening sky when Sir John entered.

'Sit down, Sir John,' Wilson said, still gazing out of the window. 'Looks as if we might get a spot of rain.'

Carson remained silent.

'I won't keep you long, Sir John,' Wilson said from the same position. 'I'd like you to tell me about your argument with Sir Edward this morning, please.'

'How . . . how . . . it wasn't really an argument,' Carson blustered. 'More a heated discussion.'

'Oh yes?' Wilson exclaimed swinging round to face the silver-haired baronet. 'Then why did you threaten him with blackmail?'

'Blackmail!' Carson exploded. 'I never did any such thing! I don't know who told you that, inspector, but. . .'

'That's none of your concern, Sir John,' Wilson interrupted. 'I know you threatened to expose the relationship between Sir Edward and his personal secretary, Carol Grayson. So please don't play around with me,' he added angrily.

'Very well,' Sir John said in a subdued voice. 'It's true. But I wouldn't have done anything about it, believe me. I was feeling desperate—I needed a contract. . .'

'The Middle East contract?'

Sir John nodded, not appearing surprised at the inspector's knowledge.

'How did you know about Sir Edward and Miss Grayson?' Wilson snapped.

'She used to work for me,' Carson replied. 'And she had been having an affair with John Thorne. There was even talk about the pair of them becoming engaged before she met Edward,' he commented wryly. 'So off she went to Edward, and Thorne, the idiot, goes and tries to make a separate deal with his cousin over this Middle East business. If you ask me, he just wanted to get Carol Grayson back.'

'So surely it would be in your best interests to have John Thorne out of the way?' the detective asked.

'You're not suggesting. . .'

'Correct. I'm not suggesting,' Wilson interceded. 'I'm surmising. Why didn't you go on the shoot?'

'I didn't feel like it,' Carson grunted. 'I was in no mood for pleasantries with Sir Edward.'

'Yet you went to the lodge,' Wilson pointed out.

'I was still discussing my business with Edward on the way, that's why.'

'Did you consider going out on the shoot at all?'

'Yes, I did.'

'Did you handle any of the guns?' Wilson asked,

working on a long shot.

'I picked up one or two from the cabinet as the others were preparing to leave,' Carson sighed.

'Thank you, Sir John, that's all for now,' the inspector said brusquely. 'But please stay in the lodge.'

'That's all?' Carson said, surprised.

'For now, yes. I'll take a full statement later. The sergeant will show you out and if you could ask Miss Grayson to pop in for a few minutes I'd be grateful.'

Carol Grayson was a 22-year-old blonde with a fine figure. Her eyes were red with crying and she was obviously in state of shock.

'I won't keep you long, Miss Grayson, 'Wilson said gently. 'Could you outline your relationship with Sir Edward?'

'I was his personal secretary,' she sniffed.

'That was your official position,' the inspector said quietly. 'What else?'

'We. . . we. . . were very close.' She was almost whispering.

'And John Thorne? What about him?'

'I finished with him when I came to work for Sir Edward. But John kept chasing me threatening to tell Lady Newby about my relationship with Edward, and how he would be in a position soon to tell Edward what to do.' She shook her head. 'It was something to do with the Middle East, I think.'

'Yes, I know about that,' said Wilson. 'Now tell me, do you know anything about guns?'

'No,' Carol said, shaking her head. 'I never went on any of the shoots.'

'Thank you. I can see you're upset. Please stay around and I'll talk to you again later.'

After Carol Grayson had left, the inspector stood up and walked over to the window where he watched the black clouds scud across the sky for about five minutes. Sergeant Stonelee stood at the door watching the detective.

Eventually Wilson nodded and returned to his seat.

'Sergeant, could you ask all the witnesses to come back again,' he said. 'And bring a couple of constables in with you. I'm going to make two arrests. One for murder and the other for conspiracy. This should be quite a case when it gets to court.'

The sergeant stared at Wilson in amazement.

'Two arrests? Who?'

The inspector smiled.

'You'll see,' he commented simply.

Well–do you *know whodunnit?*

A SPEEDY END

Tom Mitchell, like everyone else in the country, had read of the tragic death of Bobby Groves, the young motor-cycle champion. Groves, riding in the 'big bike class' had been one of Britain's shining hopes for the world title. The young rider had already won most of the British and European titles, and all that remained in terms of prestige was the World Championship. The race in the Midlands was important in terms of points, and an international list of competitors were taking part.

According to the reports Tom had read while sitting in his small office in the centre of London next door to a famous night club—the nearest he got to the so-called glamour of a private detective's life, he often said—Bobby Groves had been leading from the start. But with only four laps to go, his bike had careered out of control, hit a safety barrier and he was flung back onto the track where he died almost instantly. The race had been stopped, and still, three days later, the motor-cycle world was in a state of shock.

Special features had appeared in the newspapers; tributes to Bobby had been shown on television and an appeal fund had been started to make motor-cycling safer, a cause which had been near to Bobby's heart. All the reports had one thing in common—that 24-year-old Bobby had been a man with the world at his feet. He had recently become engaged to Tessa Wright, the beautiful film actress, and marriage was on the cards.

Mitchell had shown no more than a passing interest in the stories. But when Ted Marshall, Bobby's manager, had phoned asking him to investigate the death, he went over the reports again. Marshall had asked him to investigate Bobby's death, and Tom, with certain bills looming close, had agreed immediately.

'Why did you ask me to do the job?' he asked the manager at their first meeting. He had learned nothing at all from the reports.

'You were recommended by a freind,' Marshall replied brusquely. 'Now look, lad,' he went on. 'Whatever your fees and expenses are, I'll pay them. I want Bobby's killer found, y'hear. That boy of mine was the best in the world. I tell you, lad, he was magic. Magic. Bike racing'll never see another like him, y'hear. And now this smear campaign in this morning's press,' he added, flinging a popular newspaper across at Tom. 'They're trying to make out Bobby was a playboy! Into drugs and all that sort of rubbish! I won't have it, y'hear? I want my boy's name cleared!' he shouted, sweat breaking out on his brow.

Tom gazed at the fat man in front of him for a few seconds. They were sitting in Marshall's opulent office in Mayfair an hour after Tom had received the call from the manager.

'I know how you feel, Mr Marshall,' he said. 'But you said "Bobby's killer". What makes you so sure it wasn't an accident?'

'Because I know!' Marshall snapped. 'Bobby knew that race track like the back of his hand. He was coming round the snake bend when the bike went out of control. He'd taken that bend hundreds of times before. Hundreds,' the manager emphasised.

'Even the best of riders can make mistakes,' Tom reflected.

'Whose side are you on, anyway?' Marshall asked angrily. 'You're worse than the police who said it was "an unfortunate accident"! And even when I told them I knew the bike had been tampered with, they said I was being over-suspicious and they couldn't find anything to back me up. Mind you, they did interview nearly everyone, but I'm still not satisfied.'

'Let's get one thing straight, Mr Marshall,' Tom said drily. 'I'm not working against the police. All I'll say is that maybe they overlooked something. No police force is infallible. And that goes for me, too. So tell me why you think the bike had been tampered with?'

The manager nodded, and then shuffled some papers in front of him. Pulling out a sheet covered with handwriting, he passed it over to Tom.

'This is the report of Bob Knowles, our chief mechanic,' he explained. 'What he doesn't know about bikes isn't worth knowing about. To save you going right through it now, the most important thing is that he discovered the clutch cable wasn't properly housed into the engine.'

'What difference would that make?' Tom asked. 'I'm sorry, but the finer points of motor-bike mechanics lose me.'

'Fair enough,' Marshall conceded. 'The clutch cable runs from the handlebar on the left down to the engine, fitting into a hole which houses a sprocket, to put it simply. If the cable is not fully seated in the engine-sprocket cover-hole, then it can slip into place later and the clutch won't disengage. Follow?'

'I think so,' Tom nodded. 'That means if Bobby was entering the corner at about 90 mph, as the papers said he was, and the clutch suddenly slipped into place, he would be freewheeling into disaster.'

'You've got it, lad,' Marshall exclaimed. 'And someone made sure that clutch was out before Bobby went on that track.'

'But why didn't Knowles notice before the race?' Tom inquired.

'The sprocket's covered up, you see,' the manager explained. 'Bob would just test for position, but you could never tell. Whoever did it knew about bikes, I can tell you that much. Someone who wanted to make sure Bobby was out of racing for a long while. You see, lad, you must remember the bike could have gone out of control anywhere. The fact Bobby was killed *was* a pure accident. He might just have been hurt badly.'

'I see. Do you know if Bobby was under any pressure or threats from anyone?'

'He wasn't under no threats,' the manager replied. 'But pressure—yes. It's a tough business this, Mr Mitchell. You tend to live on your nerves most of the time. That's why you can't have any distractions like women and drinking with the lads every night. And as if Bobby didn't have enough troubles what with the World Championships coming up, he goes and gets involved with this film star, Tessa Wright.'

'Oh, so you don't approve of her, then?'

'That jumped-up trollope!' Marshall exploded. 'I've no time for her at all. Taking Bobby to all these fancy night-clubs and parties. I told him his career would suffer, but he just laughed at me. I said he would have an accident one day because he was too tired to concentrate. And that heavy manager of hers, David Blastow, always hanging around and telling Bobby to lay off his property. As if Bobby was doing the chasing!'

'Yes, yes,' Tom said, trying to calm Marshall down. 'Let's go back to before the race. Where were you the evening before?'

'In my hotel having a meeting with our sponsors,' Marshall replied. 'I was there all night.'

'You never came down to the track?'

'Oh, yes. I nipped out for ten minutes and drove over to the track, looking for Bobby.'

'You didn't know where he was?'

'No, blast it. I'd called from the hotel to see if Bobby was all right. He told me he'd be at the track most of the evening and then was going to have an early night—on my instructions,' the manager added firmly. 'But a girl answered the phone and told me Bobby had not been seen for the last hour. I was so blinking angry I jumped into my car and raced down there. The receptionist was right. Bobby

11

had not been seen, and no-one knew where he was.'

'Was the bike unattended all night, then?' Tom asked.

'Of course not!' Marshall said. 'But that's another funny thing. I looked in at the workshops and they were deserted. I'd hired this firm of security guards to watch the bike 24 hours a day on three shifts round the clock. There was no guard. I phoned the security people and they assured me a man was on that night, and he must have gone to the toilet when I popped in. Mind you, I only stayed around for a few minutes, so it could have been possible. I got my secretary to phone later and there was a man on duty, whom she spoke to.'

'Did anyone see you when you were at the track apart from the receptionist who answered the telephone?'

'Yes, in fact I bumped into Count Vallère, the financier for our leading opposition team.'

'And what was he doing?'

'Coming out of the workshops, funnily enough. Said he'd popped down to check his team's bikes. He was carrying a spanner in his hand and I joked he must be hard up to be doing his own mechanics. He said he needed it to tighten a bolt he'd discovered was loose in his car. I didn't think anything of it then. But now. . .'

'Yes, well I'll talk to him later, if necessary,' Tom interrupted. 'Out of interest, how long would it take to loosen the clutch from its housing?'

'Oh, let's see,' Marshall said slowly. 'You'd have to undo the bolt on the outside, pull the clutch out of its sprocket and tighten the bolt again with a spanner. I reckon about five minutes at the most.'

'Thank you, Mr Marshall,' Tom said. 'I think that's all for now. I'd like to chat with the security guard if possible. Do you know where I can contact him?'

'He's right here,' Marshall said smugly. 'The police questioned him in the Midlands, so I reckoned you'd want to chat with him too. When I came down to London last night I brought him with me.'

'Good thinking, Mr Marshall,' Tom commented. 'It

saves me a trip. Could you ask him to come in here, and could I possibly borrow your office for a private talk with him over the next ten minutes.'

'No trouble,' the manager muttered, standing and going to the door. 'But remember,' he added, pausing at the door, 'I want my boy's name cleared. At all costs!'

'I can only work on the truth, Mr Marshall,' Tom said, gazing directly at the manager. 'Whatever that is.'

Marshall grunted and hurried out to find the security guard.

Bert Carter was in his fifties, and looked the rugged, ex-army man he was.

'You were on the night shift the evening before the race is that right?' Tom asked, after shaking hands with the guard.

'From midnight to eight in the morning, sir,' Carter replied smartly. 'As I told the police, no-one got near that bike the night before the race without me knowing it and noting it down in my little book.'

'You kept a record?' Tom exclaimed in open admiration.

'Yes, sir,' Bert answered proudly. 'It's an old habit from my army days, when I used to do guard duty at the barracks. We had to record everyone coming or going. I remember once. . .'

'Yes, Bert,' Tom interrupted. 'You must tell me about it another time. I'd like to see that book later if I may. Was that your first shift looking after the bike?'

'Oh, no, sir. I'd been on the night shift for five days looking after the machine—ever since it was brought. It was a nice job, too, I may say. Easy.'

'You don't have your book on you now, do you?' Tom smiled.

'I do indeed, Sir,' Bert grinned, pulling a small black notebook from his side pocket. 'I thought you might like it.'

Tom took the book and opened it. It was pocket-sized and each page was ruled. On the inside cover Bert had written his name and that of the security firm. Underneath was the title, BOBBY GROVES JOB. Opposite he had drawn a line down the centre of the page. Over the left hand column he had written DATE AND TIME and, over the right, VISITORS. Above the column was printed, SATURDAY.

'Very efficient, Mr Carter,' Tom commented. 'You've got three names down here for the Saturday before the race—Tessa Wright, David Blastow and Count Vallère. Did you notice anything unusual when they appeared?'

'Not really, sir,' Carter replied. 'As I've noted, Tessa Wright came into the workshop around midnight and wanted to know if I'd seen Bobby Groves. I hadn't and told her so. She said she'd probably be at some club she mentioned and left.

'So she didn't go near the bike?'

'Not quite, sir,' Bert said. 'After speaking to me she wandered off to the back where the bike was kept, and came back in a bad mood.'

'Why was that?'

'She'd caught her dress—one of those loose, long things—on a bike she said, and would have to go home and change. The next time I saw her was at the race which I went to see.'

'Fine. What about David Blastow?'

'That's odd, sir, as I told the police,' Bert replied. 'I got this telephone call in the main building. One of the receptionists came across to fetch me. It was Ted Marshall, and we chatted and he wanted to know if everything was all right. I told him it was, and he hung up. I went back to the workshop where my little office was, and met David Blastow coming out carrying some tools. His hands were dirty with oil. He said his car'd broken down and he was borrowing the tools.'

'How long were you away altogether then?' Tom inquired.

'About ten minutes, no more. Then I stayed the rest of the night. Mr Blastow came back about fifteen minutes later—you'll see his name in the book—and returned the tools. The next day was the accident and I seem to be doing nothing but answering blinking questions since then.'

'I suppose it makes a change from the normal routine,' Tom smiled. 'Still, as you say it sounds an easy job you had. Are you interested in motor-bikes, then?'

'Me, sir?' Bert replied, raising his eyebrows. 'Cor, no, sir. I'm a cyclist—machines and me don't get along.'

'So why did you go to the race?' Tom queried.

'I had a free pass, didn't I?' Bert replied. 'And I felt sort of involved, like. I wanted to cheer the lad on.'

'Did you see the actual accident, Bert?'

'I sure did, sir,' Bert sighed deeply. 'I was on the first turn of the snake bend when Bobby comes hurtling round. It was terrible, he just seemed to lose control and went straight into the barrier. There was an almighty bang and his body was flung backwards. There was nothing anybody could do.'

'Did you see the bike when it was brought back to the workshop?'

'Yes, sir. What a bloomin' mess. The front wheel's all twisted and the handlebars pushed right back. The impact had been so bad that the front fork suspension was right up at the handlebars practically, and—you'll hardly believe this—the stem-head bolt at the top of the steering stem was pushed right out from the crash. It was a right old mess! I've never been on a motor-bike in my life and after seeing that there's no way I will go on one.'

Tom grunted and shook his head. 'It sure is a dangerous sport,' he commented. 'Before the race you didn't see anyone working on the bikes, did you?'

'Oh, just the usual mechanics,' Bert said. 'There were no suspicious characters, if that's what you mean.'

'Exactly,' Tom agreed. 'Are you staying in London for a while?'

'Yes,' Bert nodded. 'I've been given a few days off because of this business.'

'Good, I might want to talk to you again,' Tom said.

Devonshire Towers, where Tessa Wright lived, was a luxury block of flats in the West End of London. After getting the address from Marshall and telephoning, Tom had gone straight there by taxi. A man, who identified himself as David Blastow, had answered the phone, and after a bit of grumbling had agreed to see the private detective.

It was Blastow who answered the door and ushered Tom through to the front room where both men settled in large armchairs opposite one another.

'Let me say right away, Mr Mitchell,' Blastow said, 'that your questions will not be welcome. I've had enough with the police over the last three days—and so has Miss Wright. As a matter of fact Miss Wright is under sedation at the moment. The shock of her fiancé's death has been a terrible blow. But I'm sure I can answer any questions for her.'

'Mmmmm, that's too bad,' Tom muttered. 'I was hoping to have a word with Tessa myself. Anyway, it can't be helped. I gather that you and Miss Wright visited the workshops separately on the night before the race?'

'That's right,' Blastow nodded. 'Tessa went looking for Bobby and I went down for some tools.'

'Why didn't Tessa know where Bobby was?'

'They'd had a row earlier on in the evening, if you must know. As I told the police, she'd come to my hotel room in a terrible state.'

'And what did you do?'

'I'm afraid I wasn't much help to her,' Blastow admitted. 'I told her that Bobby Groves cared for nothing except his bikes and that he couldn't give a hoot if Tessa's acting career went sky-high. All Groves was interested in was having a pretty lady around him. It's no secret that I was dead set against their getting together because of Tessa's career.'

'Yes, well, I suppose I can see your point,' Tom said. 'But when did you get down to the track?'

'After Tessa left saying she was going to the track, I had something to eat and decided to follow her. But my car broke down not far from the grounds and I tinkered about with it for around fifteen minutes before giving up and going for some tools.'

'What was wrong with it?'

'Oh, the carburettor was playing up,' Blastow replied. 'I dismantled it and found the float chamber sticking. But then I discovered the distributor wasn't working properly either, so I had to take that off. That's when I went for the tools.'

'How did you dismantle the carb without tools?' Tom asked.

'I have a small tool-kit in the car, but it's limited.'

'You seem to know quite a bit about cars and engines, Mr Blastow,' Tom said. 'Where did you learn it all?'

'You may not believe it, but I used to be a car mechanic years ago, before I got the chance to get out. In fact, and this is the irony of the thing, before Tessa got involved with Bobby, both she and I were keen supporters of motor-cycle racing. We grew up in the same district, Tessa and I,' Blastow smiled. 'And used to run around in a club of motor-cyclists. Not big stuff, I add, just little bikes and we used to tinker about with them every Sunday more than ride them, to tell the truth.'

'Oh, so Miss Wright knows a little about bikes as well?'

'Certainly. She's a most amazing lady, I can tell you.'

'So I've read, Mr Blastow,' Tom smiled. 'It really is a shame I can't meet her. But let's go back to the night before the race. You got your tools okay?'

'Yes, I picked them up from the workshop. There was no one there when I went in, so I helped myself. Oh, sorry, I saw the guard in his office and waved at him, and later when I took the stuff back had a chat with him.'

'You knew where the tools were?'

'Oh, yes. I'd been down there before, you see. I spent about five minutes picking out the tools I needed and then left.'

'You didn't touch the bike?'

'Of course not! I wanted to fix my car and go and look

for Tessa.'

'Did you find her in the end?'

'Unfortunately not. The next time I saw her was later that night when I stopped off at the track to see if she was there. She was headed away from the workshop and we had another argument. She said I'd been right about Bobby and she'd just seen him in town with another girl—in fact it was the sponsor's fiancée and there was nothing to it, but she didn't know that. I ran Tessa to her hotel and we met the next day at the race. And that, Mr Mitchell, is all I can tell you, I'm afraid.'

'Oh, you've told me enough thank you, Mr Blastow,' Tom said quietly. 'I won't trouble you any more—for now.'

Ted Marshall was sitting behind his desk when Tom entered the office.

'Mr Marshall, I want you to do something for me, please,' he told the manager.

'What is it? Have you got any leads?'

Tom ignored the question but said, 'Ring Tessa Wright and David Blastow and ask them over here immediately. Give them any excuse. And ask Bert Carter to step in here in a few minutes, after I've made a phone call.'

'Certainly,' Marshall said, and he rang Tessa Wright who was still with Blastow. He then asked his secretary to get Bert Carter along to the office in five minutes.

'And now I'll make that phone call,' Tom said, dialling a number.

'Who are you calling?' Marshall asked.

'The police,' Tom answered. 'No doubt they'll be wanting to ask some further questions. But I want to warn them that they'll be making an arrest for murder.'

'You. . . you. . . don't mean you know who done it?'

Tom smiled.

'You'll see.'

Yes, Tom did know Whodunnit? There are some 'obvious' suspects here, can you pull out the right one?

OFFICE PROCEDURE

Sergeant Stanley Webb nurtured his mug of hot tea in his hands, propped his feet up on the old desk in front of him, and balanced on his chair.

'What a start to the month,' he moaned. 'First of all, it's blowing a gale outside, then my ten-year-old daughter comes in this morning with a cup of tea while I'm still in bed. That's nice, I thought, and sat up and sipped at it. I thought I was being poisoned!' he went on. 'Then my daughter starts laughing and shouting "April Fool! April Fool!" I forgot it was the First of April. What a day, *and* it's only Monday as well.'

Peter Stanstead, the young constable to whom Webb was directing his moans, tried to hide his grin. He was about to offer some sympathy when the phone rang on the sergeant's desk.

Webb listened for a few minutes, nodding and grunting, before putting the phone down.

'I told you it was going to be one of those days, lad,' he commented as he stood up. 'That was Jones Ltd, the electronics factory on the new industrial site. John Parker, the Managing Director, has just been found dead in his office with a paper knife sticking in his stomach. Grab your helmet, lad, it looks as if we've got some work on our hands.'

Webb was in charge of the three-man police 'force' in the village of Ickfield, Somerset. Twenty years in the force, he was perfectly happy with his lifestyle and had no ambitions to go to the 'big cities'.

Ickfield stood between the large towns, and as part of a Government development scheme an industrial site had been built on the outskirts of the village. Jones Ltd was one of a dozen industries attracted to the site. The small police car drew up outside the squat glass-and-chrome building.

'Can't say I knew John Parker,' Webb said as he opened the door. 'Did you?' he asked the constable.

'Nope,' Stanstead shook his head. 'One of those sort who lived in the town and only worked here. I spoke to him once or twice. Nice chap—he had that big Jaguar car, if you remember.'

They went into reception and were immediately shown up to the MD's office.

'We haven't touched anything, sergeant,' Walter Harris, the works manager, told them as he met them in the outside office, the secretary's room.

'Good, good,' Webb muttered. 'Let's see what's here, then.'

They were ushered through to a large airy office, with large picture windows on one side. Directly opposite stood a splendid antique mahogany desk. Behind the desk, on a high, black leather swivel-chair lay the body of John Parker. His feet were sticking out in front of him, his head was slumped forward on his chest, and his hands held a paper knife which was stuck into his stomach. The body was lying back in the chair, and from a distance it looked as if Parker was sleeping with his hands folded across his stomach. It was only on closer inspection that a dark patch of blood on his shirt told a different tale.

'Who discovered the body?' Webb asked.

'Sally Brown, Mr Parker's secretary,' the works manager answered. 'She came in about half-an-hour ago—that would be about half past twelve he added, glancing at the large electric clock over the door. 'He was just lying here like that. I still can't believe it.'

'Why not?' Webb asked.

'I only saw him around ten,' Harris said. 'He came over to the factory—it's just behind the offices—and we

had a chat about new orders.'

'And he seemed all right then?'

'Perfectly,' Harris nodded. 'We were talking about a new order for a big television company which was going into making transistor radios. He'd only clinched it on Friday. We make silicone chips here as you probably know, and this would be a great boost for us. John seemed on top of the world, especially as we had to fight to get the contract.'

'What'll happen now?'

'I don't know. You see, he was going to sign the final deal this afternoon. I suppose our head office in London'll take care of it.'

'And you didn't speak to Mr Parker after this morning?'

'Yes, I phoned him up. That would be about, em, ten-thirty,' Harris replied. 'I wanted a document signed. But I couldn't get a reply, so I sauntered over myself. His secretary said he was on the phone long-distance, and could I leave the document. So I did, and Sally brought it over to me just after eleven. I know the time,' the works manager continued, 'because the tea lady had just brought coffee round on the trolley.'

'Where is Miss Brown now?' Webb inquired.

'In the rest room,' Harris answered. 'She was in an awful state and took a couple of aspirins to calm her down.'

'If she's up to answering a few questions I'd like to see her.'

'I'll go and get her,' Harris said walking to the door. 'You won't want to see her in here, will you?'

'No, good point.' Webb agreed. 'Where *can* I see her?'

'There's a little conference room three doors down to your left. You can use that,' he told the policemen, and left to find Sally Brown.

'Let's see what we can find in here,' Webb said to the constable after Harris had closed the door behind him. 'And you'd better get onto Homicide immediately for fingerprints and pictures and so on,' he added. 'And could you open these blinds, please, and we'll throw some light on the subject.'

The constable nodded and walked over to the windows. He pulled a cord and slowly raised the venetian blinds. Brilliant sunlight came flooding into the room, shining directly onto the desk.

'At least that wind's blown away the clouds,' Webb muttered, carefully examining around the body. 'Well, there's nothing here that I can see,' he said, and looked carefully at the top of the desk. 'Nothing here either, except two reports, a pen and pencil set, an electronic calendar—that's nice, isn't it?—a large blotting pad and an ash-tray. Nothing else. A tidy man, our Mr Parker,' he concluded. 'You'd better ring from the secretary's office,' Webb said, walking towards the door. 'We don't want your fingerprints over the phone.'

The constable followed Webb into the small outer office. A bank of filing cabinets stood against the wall dividing it and the main office. A simple desk with three trays on it marked IN, OUT and PENDING stood against another wall opposite a few easy chairs. There was an electric typewriter on top of the desk, and a brightly coloured waste-paper basket stood on the floor to the right of the typist's chair.

Constable Stanstead began dialling.

'Looks as if he insisted on neatness in his staff as well, sir,' Stanstead commented as he tried for his number. 'Wish our office was like these,' he chuckled.

'I know what you mean,' Webb smiled. 'Mind you, I reckon we've got more paper-work than your average businessman. Look, for example, there's only two torn envelopes in the waste basket,' he pointed out and stooped to pick them up. 'London,' he muttered, looking at the postmarks. 'I'll be in the conference room,' he nodded at Stanstead, who was speaking into the phone.

The conference room contained a long table with seven chairs round it, three on either side and one at the head. Webb sat at the top and waited.

A few minutes later, a woman in her twenties, pretty

but not beautiful, entered the room. She looked as if she had been crying.

'Miss Brown, I presume,' Webb said, rising and holding out his hand.

She nodded as she shook his hand, and sat down in one of the chairs.

'I'm sorry to bother you with these questions, Miss Brown,' said Webb, sitting again. 'But we must know what happened. I'll say this, it looks like suicide, but then again it might not be. We've got to look at everything, you see.'

She smiled wanly. 'Of course.'

'Good girl,' Webb said. 'Now what time did you come into the office this morning?'

'About nine,' she replied. 'Mr Parker came in not long after.'

'And then what did you do?'

'The usual,' she replied. 'I opened the mail and took it into him. Then he told me what to do for the rest of the morning—I had to check out some records in the accounting department, which is at the other side of the building.'

'Did he strike you as being moody or depressed?' Webb asked.

'Not particularly,' Miss Brown replied. 'At least not at first. But there was one letter marked PRIVATE AND CONFIDENTIAL which he opened himself, and that seemed to put him into a bad mood.'

'Oh, yes? And do you know what was in the letter?'

'I'm sorry, but no,' she said. 'He put it in one of the drawers in his desk. He was. . .' she turned as the door opened and Constable Stanstead came in.

'Constable, could you go back to Mr Parker's office and look carefully in the drawers of his desk and try and find a letter marked PERSONAL,' Webb said.

Stanstead nodded and left.

'And now, Miss Brown,' said the sergeant gently. 'Can you tell me what happened next?'

'Before I went down to the accounts office, he asked me to put in a long-distance call to New York. It took quite a while to get through, but eventually I did it.'

'Can you remember who he was calling?'

'Yes. A Mr Salvatore Carboni. I'd got him before for Mr Parker. We were lucky because Mr Carboni had only just arrived at his office and was leaving almost immediately, his secretary told me.'

'Salvatore Carboni? Are you sure?' Webb asked, seeming puzzled. 'Think carefully, please.'

'Of course I'm sure,' Miss Brown said. 'It's such an odd name.'

'Quite right,' Webb agreed. 'And he's a very odd man. You may not know this, but he's high on the lists at Interpol and the FBI. Don't look so surprised, Miss Brown,' he said, smiling. 'Even we country policemen have to keep up with what's happening in the world. The thing is that your Mr Carboni is a suspected international swindler. This is becoming more and more interesting. Ah, here's Constable Stanstead,' he added as the policeman came into the room, carrying a sheet of paper.

'Let's see what this says,' Webb said, taking the paper by the edge and laying it on the table.

'Parker,

So you got the contract. Well done. But you know the boss told you lay off the deal. This means your payments to him are going to be increased by fifty per cent. Or else we expose your little fiddles of a few years ago when you worked these other deals for your old company. If you don't pay up then we got another kind of contract for you. Phone the boss in New York this morning.'

Webb paused after reading the letter, his face serious. 'Blackmail, very nice,' he muttered. 'It's dated yesterday, so the "boss" must be Mr Carboni. Where is the envelope for this, constable?'

'There wasn't any,' Stanstead replied. 'The letter was just lying in the drawer with some other stuff.'

'Miss Brown, do you remember what he did with the envelope?' he asked the secretary.

She shook her head.

'He might have crumpled it and put it in his pocket,' she suggested.

'Where were you when he read the letter?' Webb asked.

'Standing in front of his desk—oh, no sorry, he waved me to the side when he opened it, probably not wanting me to read it. I went to the window. I remember now. I waved to my friend—another secretary in one of the other buildings. Then Mr Parker told me to get the New York number.'

'Good, good,' Webb commented. 'Did Mr Parker have any visitors this morning?'

'Yes, he had a Mr John Mitchell from London,' she replied.

'John Mitchell? The man who was in the newspapers last year for being involved in that company fraud?'

'I. . . I. . . think so,' the secretary said. 'He came about eleven o'clock after Mr Parker had made his call. I took in Mr Harris's document for signature, made them coffee and went to the accounts department, and then came back at 12.30 to find him dead.'

'There were no other calls?'

'Yes, sorry. One. It was Mrs Parker. I put her through when Mr Mitchell was with him.'

'I don't suppose Mr Mitchell is still here, is he?' Webb inquired.

'He is, as a matter of fact,' Miss Brown said. 'He was meant to have lunch with Mr Parker. But obviously . . . anyway he's down in the factory somewhere, I believe.'

'Go find him, constable,' the sergeant said. 'I think we should have a chat with him.

'Well, I think that should be all for now from you, Miss Brown,' Webb said gently. 'You'll be very distressed, no doubt. From what I see of his office, he was a most particular man and a good boss, I would imagine.'

'Sometimes too particular,' the secretary tried to laugh. 'To think I used to moan about it as well! It makes me feel terrible now. He was so fussy for example, he insisted on using a fresh carbon for every letter.'

'That's a bit extravagant, isn't it?' Webb queried.

'That's what I used to tell him,' she said. 'In fact I said it to him this morning when we sent a letter to head office. But all he said was "People judge you by the way you treat them". In fact. . .'

She stopped suddenly as the door burst open and a smartly dressed lady in her forties rushed in.

'Is it true?' she screamed. 'My husband's committed suicide? I don't believe it!'

Webb glanced at the secretary and suggested she leave. He went across to the distraught Mrs Parker and led her to a chair.

'I was only speaking to him this morning,' she wept. 'Oh, it's all my fault, all my fault,' she moaned.

'What do you mean?' Webb asked.

'I phoned him this morning and told him I was leaving him,' she cried. 'You see, he'd been acting funny lately, going off to secret meetings which he wouldn't tell me about. I thought he was seeing another woman, and I couldn't stand it. This had been going on for about three months and at the weekend he was out all Saturday night and didn't come home until after lunch on Sunday,' she wept.

'Didn't your husband give you any idea of what he was doing?'

'He said he was having important business meetings with people in London. I found his diary once and there was this name, J. Mitchell. I thought it was his girl friend but he said it was a man. Well, I said this morning I'd had it up to my eyes, and was leaving this afternoon. And then I got the call saying he was dead.'

'Well, this is a turn-up for the books,' Webb mumbled. 'Perhaps you should go and rest and we'll chat later, okay?'

The sergeant accompanied Mrs Parker to the door and opened it for her. Constable Stanstead was standing there with a man wearing a dark suit and carrying a brief-case.

'Come in, Mr Mitchell,' he said, noting the look of surprise and shock on Mrs Parker's face. 'I think we'd better talk.'

As soon as Mitchell was in the room he said, 'I'm not saying anything until I speak to my lawyer. I've had enough of you lot, what with that case last year,' he added.

'I wouldn't take that attitude, if I were you, Mr Mitchell,' Webb said. 'No one is accusing you of anything. I just want some information from you. Like what your meeting was about this morning with Mr Parker.'

'That's none of your business!' Mitchell snapped. 'It was personal!'

'Okay. Do you know a Salvatore Carboni?' Webb asked.

Mitchell's expression of shock and amazement told the sergeant he had hit home.

'What . . . what . . . what's that to do with it?' he stammered. 'Sure, I know him. Lotsa people do. You're not going to pin this on me, y'hear? No way.'

'I'm not trying to, Mr Mitchell,' Webb said smiling. 'Of course it would be a clever move on your part to stay around as if you didn't know anything about it. But apart from that how long were you with Mr Parker?'

'About forty minutes, from eleven to about quarter to twelve,' Mitchell said quietly. 'Then I went for a walk.'

'A walk?' Webb echoed incredulously.

'Yeah, I had this headache and wanted to clear it before lunch. I went as far as the next factory. I popped into Parker's factory and then I heard about John.'

'The next factory . . .,' Webb said slowly. 'Let me see . . . that's Modern Electronics, isn't it?'

Mitchell nodded. 'I'm not saying anything more until I speak to my lawyer,' he said sullenly.

'I'm sure you're not,' Webb said. 'The fact that two rival electronics firms are beside each other is odd enough, but the fact you visited both is odder still,' he added. 'Constable Stanstead, please ensure this man stays on the premises until the detectives arrive!'

'You can't keep me here!' protested Mitchell.

'You're wanted for further questioning,' Webb said simply.

The constable left with Mitchell, who was still demanding to speak to his lawyer. A few minutes later, Stanstead was back.

'I had to lock him in a store cupboard,' the constable explained. 'I'm sure it's not strictly proper, but I don't think he'll complain about that, do you?'

'I don't think that type would really complain about anything that brought attention to themselves. Mind you, he might moan later, when the facts are known.'

'Well sarge, murder or suicide?' the constable asked.

'Just think, lad, just think!' Webb smiled. 'You can answer this question yourself'.

Can you? Was *it suicide or murder? If murder, then Whodunnit? Webb's opinion can be seen in the answer section.*

THE FINAL CURTAIN

Sergeant Bond looked at the two constables standing beside a tarpaulin on the stage of the deserted theatre.

'Are you going to start singing "A Policeman's Lot is Not a Happy One"?' he quipped as he walked towards them.

'No, sir,' they both replied humourlessly.

'Just a joke,' Bond said as he bent down and lifted the corner of the sheet.

The body of Nigel Osborne, leading man in the Corner Theatre's production of *Moonlight Passion,* lay with a knife sticking out of its heart. A dark patch of blood had spread, staining the medieval costume Osborne was wearing.

'How long has he been like this?' he asked one of the policemen.

'Since just before the final curtain!' a voice boomed from the right of the stage. 'Approximately 10.15.'

Bond turned and saw a tall, well-built man wearing a blue open-necked shirt, a silk cravat and dark blue trousers striding towards him.

'John Trent, director,' the man said, holding out his hand to the rising detective. 'A ghastly accident, but if there's anything my cast or I can do to help you, just ask,' he added, shaking Bond's hand firmly.

'That's very kind of you,' the sergeant said. 'But does that mean you don't think it was an accident?'

'I'm convinced it was, officer,' Trent said in a confident voice. 'But no doubt you'll need all the facts for the coroner. When I directed *Murder in the Priory,* I studied police procedure. . .'

'I'm sure you did,' Bond interrupted. 'But tell me why you said it was "a ghastly accident"?'

'I don't know if you're familiar with the play, *Moonlight Passion,*' said Trent, and he received his answer from the expression on Bond's face. 'In the final act the hero—played by Nigel—is killed by the heroine before she takes her own life,' the director explained. 'We use a dummy knife in which the blade goes back into the handle for the scene. Tonight the blade must have stuck as it went straight into Nigel's heart as you can see. A terrible accident. I doubt my wife will ever recover from it.'

'Your wife?' Bond said.

'Yes, she was playing the heroine. She did the actual stabbing,' Trent told the detective.

'Terrible, terrible,' Bond sympathised.' So she brought the knife on to the stage?' he asked.

'No, Nigel carried it in his belt,' Trent said. 'It is a most dramatic moment when he pulls the knife out and says "My life is not worth living. I have to . . ."'

'Yes, yes, I can imagine,' Bond muttered. 'Where was Osborne before he came on to the stage?'

'In his dressing room,' Trent replied. 'He's on for most of the second act.'

'Good, let's go and see his dressing room now,' Bond suggested, walking to the right of the stage.

'Eh, this way, please,' the director said, waving his arm to the left of the stage. 'Nigel's dressing room is over here.

They went into the side-wings where the detective noticed a chair.

'What's that for?' he asked.

'The prompter's chair. She reads the play while the actors are on stage. In case they forget their lines she shouts them out,' Trent explained.

'I see,' said Bond, and he followed the director down a passage. Half-way down on the left, there was a door with DRESSING ROOM 1 written on it. Trent c

'This was Nigel's room,' he said, stepping allow the detective to pass.

The dressing room was fairly small and cloth scattered over several chairs. Directly opposite as they walked in was another door with wardrobes at either side. A mirror ran half-way along the right wall, surrounded by naked bulbs which shone brightly. In front of the mirror was a small counter with a lighted, slightly perfumed candle on it, and to the right of the candle stood a single rose in a tall glass.

The detective sergeant went over to the flower and sniffed it. 'Very pleasant,' he muttered, picking up a small ball of candle grease which had fallen beside the rose, and twirling it between his fingers. 'Where does that door lead to?' he asked, pointing in between the wardrobes.

'Round the back of the stage,' said Trent. 'It's another entrance, and means entries can be made from right of stage.'

'This is rather a plush place for an amateur dramatic society, isn't it?' Bond claimed.

'You're quite right,' Trent laughed. 'We just borrowed it.'

'I think that's all in here,' Bond said. 'I noticed there was a little office as I came in. I'll use that now,' he added, moving to the door into the main passage. As he was passing a chaise longue opposite the mirror he pointed at it.

'Osborne was a photographer?' he asked, indicating a camera lying on it, and a flash attachment with a used bulb.

'Oh, no, that's Debby's—my wife's' Trent answered. 'She always takes pictures of the cast on the last night for our scrap book.'

Trent would not leave Bond's side as the men headed for the office. That did not bother the detective so much as the director's incessant chatter. Finally, when both men were sitting in the small office, Bond stared at Trent.

'I'm sure what you're saying about theatre and safety

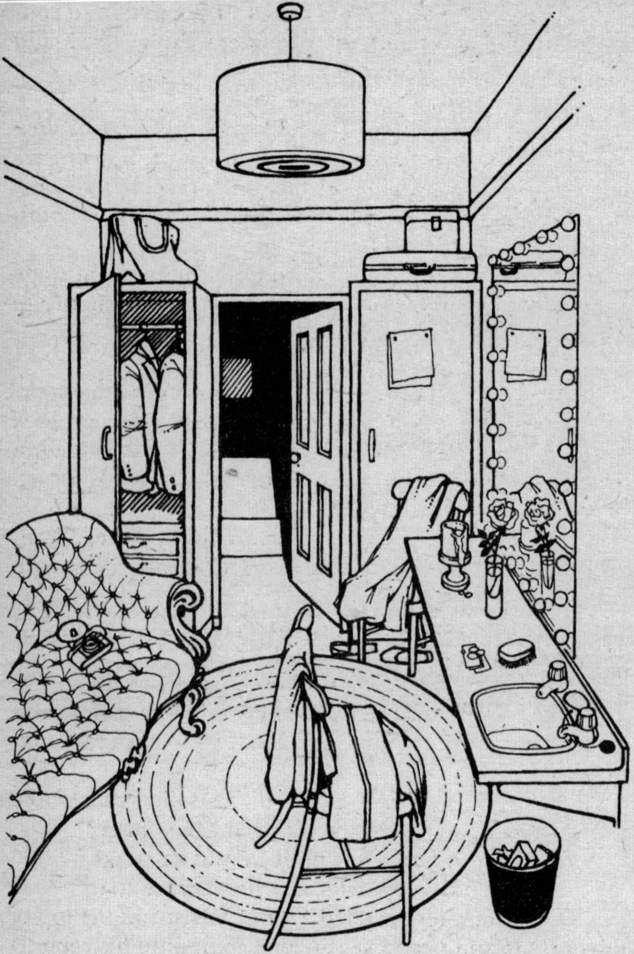

precautions is true, Mr Trent,' he said. 'But there's a man lying dead on the stage now. When did you last see him apart from on the stage?'

'At the interval,' Trent replied. 'I popped in to congratulate him and point out a couple of things he should emphasise in the second act.'

'Did the two of you get on well?'

'As individuals, yes, I would say,' the director answered. 'But as director and actor, not so well. You see, we had our own ideas about the theatre and sometimes this would reach boiling point. Nothing personal in it, we both realised, just artistic difference,' he claimed.

'Where was the knife before Osborne went on stage with it?' Bond asked quickly before Trent had a chance to go on about art and the theatre.

'In Nigel's dressing room of course.'

Bond glanced at the constable standing at the door.

'Constable, could you go and have a thorough look round Mr Osborne's dressing room. You're looking for a dummy knife similar to the one that killed Mr Osborne,' he said.

'Oh, I'm sure you won't find anything there,' Trent said. 'In fact, I put the dummy knife in Nigel's sheath when I was chatting with him.'

'You did, did you?' Bond asked sharply. 'And then what did you do with the sheath?'

'Laid it on the dressing table—just beside his candle and rose,' Trent answered. 'He always had a candle and rose when he was acting,' he added, by way of explanation.

'No doubt,' commented Bond. 'And then you left the dressing room and didn't see him until on stage?'

'That's it, officer. Not until he was on stage.'

'Who would know who saw him before that?'

'The prompter,' replied Trent. 'She sits at the top of the passage and would see anyone going into his room.'

'Could you ask her to come along here, please?'

Lucy Arnold was in her early twenties, with mousy brown hair tied at the back. She was wearing a loose jumper and denims, and fidgeted nervously as the detective spoke to her.

'Yes, yes, I could see who was going in and out of Nigel's dressing room,' she said in answer to Bond's first queston. 'Of course, there were times when I would be reading and wouldn't notice,' she added. 'I went back to my seat not long before the second act,' she went on, without waiting for Bond's further questions. 'I saw John Trent go in, and as I wanted to ask him something, I rushed down the corridor to try and catch him. But by the time I got there, he was inside. I knocked on the door and Nigel let me in. He was in his underwear getting ready to change. John was sitting on the couch with the dummy knife in his hand. I asked him a couple of questions and left.'

'Did you see anyone else go into the room?' Bond asked.

'I'll . . . I'll have to think,' Lucy said. 'Yes, there was Kate Osborne, Nigel's wife. She went in just as the second act started and must have been there about five minutes. Kate is stage-managing the production,' she explained. 'And then there was Sue Martin, the wardrobe lady, who just popped in and out. Oh, and of course, there was Debby Trent! She was going around taking pictures of everyone, and after taking one of me, she went in to Nigel. That would be sometime during the interval, I'm not sure when,' Lucy concluded.

'And you didn't see Nigel Osborne again from the time in the dressing room until he was ready to go on stage?'

'That's right,' Lucy replied. 'He came and stood beside me before going on. He'd been called by one of the stage hands exactly ten minutes before his cue.'

'I see,' the detective nodded. 'And he stayed in the wings for a few minutes before going on?'

Lucy nodded.

'He went on with a scroll tucked into his belt,' she said. 'As he was pushing it in, his knife dropped and I picked it up for him.'

'You picked it up?' Bond said in despair. 'Well, there's no point in looking for fingerprints on that. . .'

'Excuse me, sir.' It was the constable, who had just come back from searching the dressing room. 'Is this what you were wanting?' he asked, as he handed over a knife to the sergeant.

Bond picked up the knife by the tip. It had a large wooden handle which the detective pressed into the desk. The blade retracted into the hilt.

'Exactly, constable. Well done,' he said. 'Now we know the knives were switched. Lucy, who's in charge of props like this?'

'The stage manager, Kate Osborne,' she replied.

'Thank you, Lucy, that's all for now,' Bond said. 'Do you think Mrs Osborne is up to answering a few questions?'

'I'll find her and ask,' Lucy said as she left the office.

Kate Osborne arrived a few minutes later, visibly shaken.

'Before you ask me any questions, officer,' she started, 'I can tell you who killed my husband.'

'You can?' Bond said in amazement.

'Yes,' she nodded. 'John Trent. He'd threatened to do it before and I heard him again tonight tell Nigel he would get him.'

'Why?'

'Because of Debby Trent,' Mrs Osborne replied flatly. 'John thought they were becoming too friendly—I don't know how much truth there was in it—and Nigel denied it. Anyway, last night she and Nigel went for a meal to discuss the play. I didn't mind, but John saw red. When I went to Nigel's dressing room tonight I heard him and John arguing. That was when John threatened to kill Nigel unless he kept away from Debby.'

'Do *you* think there was any truth in the allegation?'

'What? Between Nigel and Debby?' she retorted with a smile. 'She was chasing him, that's for sure. Everyone in the cast knew that. But I wasn't worried, if that's what you mean.'

'I see,' Bond muttered. 'So you didn't actually have a chance to see your husband tonight before the second act?'

'Oh, yes. I heard John slam the other door in Nigel's room and went in. Nigel was in an awful state and said he would never work with John or Debby Trent again as they were nothing but trouble. I calmed him down and had to leave after that to attend to the play.'

'Did you see the knife at all?'

'Yes, on the chaise longue,' she replied. 'I tested it was working. And then I left it by the other door.'

'Can you remember if the knife was in its sheath?' Bond queried.

'I . . . I think so,' Mrs Osborne replied. 'Yes, it was, now I remember.'

'That's helpful,' the detective commented. 'I won't trouble you further, Mrs Osborne. Do you know where Debby Trent is at the moment?'

'In her dressing room with John, I think'

'Thanks. Constable, could you ask Debby Trent to spare me a few minutes?'

The constable left and returned almost immediately with Mrs Trent. She was a pretty woman in her mid-twenties, with a fine figure and an air of confidence about her which came through her obvious distress.

'Oh, it's terrible,' she said softly. 'I actually killed him. I feel like a murderess,' she moaned.

'I understand,' said Bond. 'But I think this was planned and you were perhaps used as a tool. There's just a few questions I want to ask you, if you don't mind. You went in to see Nigel Osborne during the interval, I believe?'

'I went to take his photograph,' Debby nodded. 'I always do that for the scrap book.'

'And did you get your picture?' Bond asked.

'Oh, yes,' she said. 'Just the one I wanted, of Nigel leaning on his make-up counter with the lights shining all around. He looked like . . . like an angel,' she said and began to cry.

Bond waited until she had settled down again.

'And you left your camera in the dressing room?'

'Yes,' she said almost inaudibly. 'I was so pleased at getting my picture, I forgot it in my excitement. I helped Nigel into his costume and then went for some coffee.'

'Which way did you leave the room?'

'The back entrance to the stage,' she said.

'And when exactly was this?'

'Just before the start of the second act,' she replied.

'And you didn't see him after that?'

'Yes, I did,' she said. 'I was on stage for about fifteen minutes and then came off. I smoked a cigarette in my dressing room and then popped along to see Nigel to wish him luck for our final performance in the play together as it was the last night,' she added. 'That was about ten minutes before he went on stage. I know because he received his call as I stood at the door.'

'You spoke to him at the back door?'

Debby nodded.

'Can you remember if you saw his knife, or rather the stage knife?'

'It was lying on the make-up counter. I remember because I said it was a shame he didn't have it there when I took the picture as it would have been a nice dramatic touch.'

Bond smiled.

'You are obviously a talented artist to notice these fine details,' he said. 'Didn't you ask him to pose again?'

'No, we were due on in about ten minutes, and anyway, he had just finished putting on some more stage make-up and the smell of the paraffin we use was driving me mad. So I wished him luck and left.'

'So the next time you met was on stage?'

'Please, officer, don't remind me,' she said, beginning to weep again. 'It's so upsetting.'

Bond glanced at the constable standing by the door.

'Please accompany Mrs Trent back to her dressing room', he said. 'And thank you Mrs Trent, I appreciate your help.'

The detective sergeant strolled out of the office after Mrs Trent had left. He went back to the dressing room used by the dead man. By now police fingerprints experts and photographers were busy there, and he leaned against the door watching them.

'Hello, Charlie,' he said to one of the men. 'Make sure you get plenty of prints and pictures. We're going to need them for the court.'

'You mean you know who did it?' Charlie asked.

'You could say that, Charlie boy,' Bond smiled. 'You could say that.'

Again lots of conflicting stories. Bond did know Whodunnit? Do you?

EQUATION OF MURDER

It was as perfect a peaceful country setting as could have been witnessed in the paintings of Constable. The old, rambling house, the green fields and woods stretching for miles around and the maze of small country paths—it was in this corner of rural England that some of the leading scientists in the world had gathered for a top-level medical conference, to compare notes, give speeches and generally try to prove that in the world of science, political barriers did not exist.

Apart from scientists, representatives of the largest chemical companies were also present. But in terms of press coverage the conference was called 'low-key', because it was not 'open'. Attendance was by invitation only, and the British Government had provided strictest security for the delegates. It was impossible to enter Wildwood Hall, the meeting place, or its large acreage of ground, without a pass. An electric fence surrounded the grounds and security guards patrolled the perimeters day and night.

So the world did not take much notice of the group of men, leaders in their fields, whose contributions to science and technology had done so much to change the face of modern life.

But suddenly Wildwood Hall was to become the centre of world attention, splashed across the front pages of practically every newspaper, when it became the scene of a bizarre death. For the man killed was none other than

Professor Terence Blumhoffen, the Nobel Peace Prize winner who was responsible for a major breakthrough in cancer research.

At first it was thought that the Professor had been the victim of a ghastly accident, but when Peter Brown, formerly with Scotland Yard's Flying Squad and now the head of security at Wildwood Hall, started to make some inquiries, he began to think differently. . .

'I've gathered you all here,' said Brown to the small group of people assembled in the large library of Wildwood Hall, 'because every one of you saw the late Professor today before he died. I've already contacted the police and because of the international nature of the case, they're sending down a team from Special Branch. But I'd like to get some preliminary information before they arrive.'

The four people present—three men and woman—gazed at the security chief. They were an odd bunch—a scientist, Otto Wingarten, who despite his name was, like Blumhoffen, an American citizen; Stella Blumhoffen, the wife of the dead man; Edward Kelly, the chairman of International Pharmaceuticals; and Tom Pritchard, a leading industrialist and friend of the late professor.

'Now, here are the facts as I know them,' Brown continued. 'If any are wrong, please tell me later. As it's Sunday, a day of relaxation had been organised. Bridge games, country walks and a rabbit shoot. Professor Blumhoffen, whose hobby in the States, I gather, is hunting and fishing, went on the rabbit shoot. As did you, Mr Wingarten and also you, Mr Pritchard,' he said looking at the two men. 'Is that correct?'

The men nodded.

'Now you'll remember,' Brown went on, 'that just before you left this morning on the shoot at about nine-thirty, we received word from the local police that a rabid dog was on the loose in the area and there was a chance it might be headed this way. I personally warned the shooting party of this, and left it up to them if they wanted to continue with the shoot. You'll recall that a few members of the group decided to stay in the Hall.'

Everyone nodded and Edward Kelly muttered something about wishing everyone had stayed.

'Those who left went down to Highridge Woods a few miles south of the Hall where the shoot was going to take place. The party—seven of you including two gamekeepers and one of my own men—became separated. My man tells me there was some shooting and it was actually he who discovered the body. As a matter of fact, I think we'd better have him in here,' he added, picking up an internal phone and speaking into it. A few minutes later a tall, broad man, who looked every inch an ex-policeman, entered the room and sat beside the others.

'Thanks, Alec,' Brown said. 'We're just running over the facts. You found the body, didn't you? For everyone's benefit, and especially mine, could you describe the circumstances?'

'Well, as you know the group somehow got split up,' Alec Jones said. 'I stayed with one of the gamekeepers. We heard some shooting around us, and I suggested we separate and try to get the party together again. I was walking through the woods when I came to a clearing. There I found Professor Blumhoffen's body lying face down, near the edge of the clearing, his hands stretched out in front of him near the edge of the clearing. Shocked, I turned him over and saw a red patch just above his heart. I checked for pulse, but he was dead. I turned him over again and saw there was a small red patch of blood in his back. I called for the gamekeepers who then rounded up the rest of the party before we returned.'

'Yes, there's no doubt about it,' said Brown. 'We now know that Blumhoffen was shot. Fortunately, he didn't suffer, according to the doctor who examined him. A bullet had entered the poor man through his kidneys at the back and gone straight through his heart and out the other side. According to the medic, he wouldn't even have known he was hit. I'm sorry, Mrs Blumhoffen, I know this is painful for you,' he commented, seeing the professor's wife flinch at the details. 'But if it's any consolation, he didn't feel any pain.'

He paused for a few moments before continuing. 'Right, I'll start with you, Mr Pritchard,' he finally said. 'Can you tell me what happened?'

'Well, as you said, we set off from here and got to Highridge Woods around ten-thirty,' said the businessman. 'We saw a pack of rabbits and started moving in on them. The pack scattered and that's when we became separated as we all went after them. I heard some shots, and I potted a couple myself. I was on my own but then I heard one of the gamekeepers calling my name and returned to the scene of the death with him. That's it.'

'How long had you known Professor Blumhoffen?' Brown asked.

'Oh, for years,' Kelly replied. 'I met him first of all in America. I wanted him to come and work for International Pharmaceuticals, my company, but he refused. Said he was better suited for pure research.'

'But if I remember it from the files I get on delegates attending conferences, there was an industrial espionage case a few years back in which you and the late professor were involved. That's so, isn't it?'

Kelly looked embarrassed, but reluctantly nodded.

'And if I remember further, Blumhoffen was meant to supply you with various pieces of information on which the US Government had sponsored the research,' Brown continued. 'In the end, while the case was not proven, you stated in court that you had paid Blumhoffen a lot of money for the information, but that he had decided in the end not to give it to you.'

'Exactly,' Kelly said vehemently. 'But no one broke the law. The money was never traced, so my story didn't stand up.'

'So it could be said you had a long-standing grudge against Blumhoffen, Mr Kelly.'

'Yes, but you're not suggesting. . .'

'Certainly not, Mr Kelly,' the security man said, smiling sweetly. 'But let's just say you had a very good motive for killing the professor.'

'Never heard anything so ridiculous in my life!' Kelly muttered. 'You can't pin this on me.'

'We shall see,' said Brown. 'Now, Mr Pritchard, you're an old friend of the deceased, aren't you?'

'Yes, that's right,' Tom Pritchard agreed. 'We went to university together in this country before Terry went out to the States. We studied medicine and chemistry, and I went straight into industry.'

'And you never had any quarrels with him?'

'None whatsoever,' Pritchard shook his head emphatically.

'Not even over the money he owed you?' Brown asked, smiling.

'How did you know about that?' the industrialist asked in surprise.

'It would amaze you the lengths security goes to when someone starts working for the Government,' Brown said. 'You did lend Blumhoffen a large amount of money some time ago, didn't you. What was it for?'

'Perhaps I shouldn't be saying this, but Terry, apart from being a brilliant scientist, was also more down-to-earth than many of his colleagues,' Pritchard claimed. 'He enjoyed the so-called good life—gambling, buying trinkets like gold and diamonds and going to night-clubs. He got into a lot of debt and asked me to help him out, which I did.'

'Have you had any of the money back?'

'Not a cent.'

'And did you know the professor was heavily insured?'

'Of course,' Pritchard replied quickly. 'We were still close friends. In fact, I was the one who arranged for a friend of mine to insure Terry.'

'Finally, Mr Pritchard, what were you and Professor Blumhoffen arguing about last night in the garden after dinner?'

Pritchard really did look amazed this time, and hesitated before answering. 'The money,' he said almost inaudibly. 'You see, I need it right now, but Terry said he couldn't get it for me immediately. Not that he was short, but he had most of his funds tied up in Switzerland, and for some reason couldn't touch it for a few years.'

A couple more things, sorry,' said Brown. 'You're an expert gunman, I'm told.'

The industrialist nodded.

'And where exactly were you when you heard the gamekeeper call your name?'

'About a couple of minutes away from the clearing.'

'That was handy. Had you actually been in the clearing before?'

'Yes. I crossed it, but saw nothing, so went back into the woods.'

'And you never saw the professor?'

'I said I saw no-one,' Pritchard repeated angrily.

'Quite, quite,' Brown said. 'But you must admit you have an excellent motive. When the professor's insurance came through, as a debtor you could claim the money—the money you need so badly.'

'I wish you'd stop playing at Sherlock Holmes, Mr Brown,' Pritchard snapped. 'Why not wait for the police to arrive?'

Brown ignored the comment.

'After the party became separated, did you meet anyone between then and when the body was discovered?'

Pritchard looked down before answering. Then glancing at Stella Blumhoffen, he shrugged and looked back at the security man.

'Yes, I did,' he sighed. 'I wasn't going to mention it, but no doubt it'll all come out. After I crossed the clearing and went into the woods, I heard a couple of shots behind me, and reckoned it was one of the party. I turned to go back to the clearing, when I ran into Stella, or rather she ran into me.'

'Exactly what do you mean, please?' the ex-detective queried.

'Stella was running away from the clearing,' Pritchard explained. 'She was in a terrible state. I could see she had been crying. She was carrying a rifle in one hand and literally almost knocked me down when I came out from behind a bush. I tried to calm her down, and asked her what had happened. She said she'd had an argument with Terry—but didn't tell me about what—and had almost killed him.'

'Almost?' Brown interceded quickly.

'So she said,' said Pritchard quietly. 'I've known them both for years and knew their marriage wasn't going well. I'm sorry Stella,' he added, turning quickly to the professor's wife. 'She said she was pointing the gun at him, when it had gone off, missing him narrowly. She was so frightened, she ran away.'

Brown glanced at Stella Blumhoffen who was sobbing softly, her face covered by her hands. 'I'll come back to that in a moment, when Mrs Blumhoffen has composed herself,' he said. 'Perhaps you can answer a couple of points for me, now, Mr Wingarten?'

'Of course, of course,' the scientist replied.

'Good. You've known the late professor a long time also, haven't you?'

'We worked together for many years,' Wingarten said. 'In fact we were on the same team that discovered the cancer breakthrough.'

'Ah, yes, I remember reading something about that,' said Brown. 'You were very bitter about Blumhoffen being given the Nobel Peace Prize, weren't you?'

'It's a long time ago now,' Wingarten sighed. 'But yes, I was upset. As I said at the time, I felt it was my own researches that led to the major discoveries. And yet I was not even acknowledged when the results were announced. All I had was a mere mention as being part of the team. I thought Terry had taken the preliminary results to the Government without telling the rest of us, thus making sure of his place in history.'

'Yes, but I don't want to go into all that here,' Brown said. 'But it is a fact, is it not, that you and Professor Blumhoffen ceased to be friends. You wouldn't speak to him, or reply to his letters. In fact, it was only

Wingarten's alleged viewpoint from the rise over the clearing.

when you both came to Wildwood that you took up your old friendship.'

'Well, I thought there was no point in going on as we were,' the scientist said, a slight smile on his face. 'I mean, scientists are meant to be above that sort of thing. And as we were both working in similar fields it seemed crazy not to pool our resources as it were.'

'Fair enough. Now can you tell me what happened to you on the shoot?'

Wingarten breathed in deeply.

'Yes, of course. But before I do, Mr Brown, I have to tell you something,' he said. 'There was no murder. Terry's death was an accident. I know, and after I've told you what happened to me, you'll see what I mean.'

'Go on,' the security chief muttered.

'Well, as you know we were all split from one another,' the scientist began.' I wandered off after some rabbits I'd seen. I kept my rifle in front of me, remembering your warning about the crazy dog on the loose.

'I saw a rabbit ahead of me and I started following it. It went up one of those ridges—a small hill, in fact—and soon I was at the top. It was possible to see into the woods from above from where I was, and I looked around, hoping to catch sight of the rest of the party. I could see directly into the clearing.' He paused for a few moments, and the room was heavy with silence.

'In the centre of the clearing a dog sat panting. I looked through my binoculars at the beast and saw the telltale marks of rabies—the foam at the mouth, the difficulty in breathing and so on. As I watched, it began to walk towards the edge of the clearing. Through my binoculars I saw a movement at the side and swung the glasses round to see Terry coming out of the woods. I yelled, but he didn't hear me. The dog began to move faster towards Terry, and he saw it, but too late. He was actually in the clearing when it pounced. He avoided it and swung round grabbing it by the throat. It wasn't a particularly big animal, so he could hold it at arm's length. But through my binoculars I could see he was going to drop it,' Wingarten went on in a quiet, sober voice. 'The dog was squirming and snapping, and Terry kept whirling round to keep his balance. I knew he would fall, so taking a chance I aimed my rifle at the dog and fired. Unfortunately, I missed the animal which scampered off, and hit Terry instead.'

Everyone in the room stared with shock at Wingarten.

'Why didn't you tell me immediately?' Brown asked.

'I was going to, but you called us all here as soon as we returned. So you see, it was a horrible accident. In trying to save Terry's life, I killed him,' Wingarten concluded, his voice faltering.

'That seems to be it, Mr Brown,' Edward Kelly said.

'Not quite, Mr Kelly,' Brown said. 'I just want to ask Mrs Blumhoffen a couple of questions.'

'Oh, come on now,' Kelly snapped. 'Aren't you carrying this a bit far? You can see the state she's in.'

'Yes, but the police'll want to question her, and if I can give them any information, it might delay their questioning.'

'I'll answer anything you want to know,' Stella Blumhoffen said firmly.

'Thank you,' Brown said. 'This is going to be painful, I know, but believe me it's best we know everything. Your marriage to the professor was not everything it should have been, was it?'

'You could put it that way,' Stella answered, smiling ruefully. 'As Tom has said. Terry enjoyed the high life. Which included women, by the way. Lately he had taken on a new laboratory technician, a young girl, and was spending a lot of time with her,' Stella said. 'That's what our argument was about. I couldn't take it any more, and wanted a divorce. Terry said he would never do that as the scandal could finish him. I was waving my gun at him when it went off.'

'Where was this?' the security man asked.

'At the edge of the clearing, near where he was

found,' Stella replied.

'And you didn't see any of this, Mr Wingarten?' Brown asked, turning to the scientist.

'No, this must have happened before the dog arrived,' Wingarten answered, stony-faced.

'Why wouldn't your late husband give you a divorce, Mrs Blumhoffen?'

'Because. . . because I wanted to marry Otto Wingarten,' she said simply.

'And did you threaten to kill your husband during the course of the argument?'

'Yes.'

'And wouldn't you say you had every intention of killing him, and that you and Mr Wingarten hatched this story of the accident up between you?'

'Certainly not!' Wingarten burst out. 'This is. . .'

He was interrupted by a security guard entering the room and going across to Peter Brown and whispering something in his ear.

'Thank you, John,' said Brown. 'I've just been informed that the bullet which killed Professor Blumhoffen has been found. Unfortunately it fits the rifles you were all carrying, which you took from the gun room. But I'm sure when Special Branch arrive and match up the ballistics, they'll be able to tie it in with the culprit's rifle. . .'

'But we've put them all back in the gun room!' Pritchard exclaimed.' And I personally slotted them all in the rack, after wiping them down.'

'That was clever,' Brown commented drily.

'I. . . I never thought,' Pritchard apologised.

'Anyway, it doesn't matter now,' Brown smiled. 'When the police arrive, I'll be able to tell them who to arrest.'

Your final Whodunnit *then!*

ANSWERS

A CASE OF SUICIDE?

Amateur Sherlock Holmeses amongst you will have noticed that there was no way Sir Michael's death could have been suicide. The body was found next to an open window which faced north-west. As there had been a storm that night. Mollé was quite right to have realised that the rain (falling in a westerly direction—remember McNee's story?) would have blown through the broken pane of glass on to the right side of Sir Michael's face. But there was a dried 'trickle' of blood running down the corpse's face on to his collar. If the body had been there all night (and the doctor said that Sir Michael had been dead 'four or five hours', making the time of death about 2.30), the blood would have spread. So the body had to have been moved to its final position.

Secondly, Mollé had noticed the cartridge from the automatic pistol lying beside the left foot of the body. But automatic pistols eject their cartridges from the right, in a backwards movement, so the cartridge should have been lying *to the right* of the body. Again, the shell must have been placed there to make it look like suicide. You can see both these points clearly in the illustration.

Thirdly, Sir Michael's suicide note was perfectly typed—a man in his position would be used to a secretary typing his letters, so he would surely have made some mistakes.

It was Dr Stanley Jenkins who gave the game away when he said he had been asked to 'make legal' the changes in the amended will. It takes *two* witnesses to make any document legal, and when he had said 'the two of us sat in the study', he was referring only to Sir Michael and himself.

In fact it was the doctor who killed Sir Michael after Algernon had left the greenhouse. Remember, McNee said he had seen Algernon there first and then the doctor.

So Mollé was able to piece the clues together from the story. And when Jenkins said he wrote short stories for publication, this almost certainly meant he could type. The nephew's wet hair and the actor's cold were red herrings!

The only thing Mollé did not know was the motive, which came out later. Jenkins had been witness to the first will, in which Sir Michael was to have left the house and some of the grounds to *him* to open a private clinic. But when Sir Michael called the doctor the second time, he told him he had changed his mind because the house had been with the family for hundreds of years. Jenkins wanted Sir Michael dead before he could change the original will.

Did you guess it?

A CURSE ON THE PHARAOH'S ROD

The first thing the Chief Superintendent did was to look at the most obvious suspects and see if their motivation was strong enough to commit a crime. The prime suspect, of course, was the Egyptian, Ahmid. Not only did he have superstitious beliefs, he had been given a tour of the museum a month before, so he knew about the security system. But what long-term good would the robbery do Ahmid? If the sceptre re-appeared in Egypt, then he would be arrested and lose his job and standing with the Egyptian Government. On top of that, his alibi did stand up.

With Peter Haskins retiring in only a few months, it was conceivable that he was putting away a 'nest-egg' for the future. He could have stolen the sceptre during the six hours the alarm system was off, but there is little doubt that its disappearance would have been noticed by the night shift. It would have been too risky and obvious if he had done it. So Brownlee dismissed Haskins as the culprit.

John Mackay's story about the torch seemed odd, but in fact was true. If he had been guilty, he would have been seen in the corridor by Arthur Mason and the Professor, who were in the vicinity just before the lights went out. So Mackay was innocent.

Arthur Mason was undoubtedly a prime suspect. He could have taken the key when he discovered the Guard Room empty.. But by his own admission—and further checking—he did not know the lay-out of the museum well enough to go through the dark so quickly and return to the Guard Room in time, after opening the outside door and passing the sceptre to an accomplice outside. And John Mackay, back in the room, would have seen Mason put the outside door key back again. Mason was 'clean', as they say in the force.

Professor Bartholomew said he met Mason in the corridor when the guard was returning from the kitchen with two mugs of tea. The Professor had just passed the Guard Room and noticed it was empty. He also said he spent ten minutes in the kitchen, preparing his cup of tea. But Mason had just made tea, so the water would still be hot. There was no way Professor Bartholomew needed ten minutes in the kitchen. In fact, he quickly made a cup of tea, and checked the Guard Room, which was empty. Taking the control key, he threw the switches, dashed to the Exhibition Room, took out the sceptre, came back via the main hall, and with his own key opened the side door to make it look as if someone had passed the rod outside. Returning to the corridor, he found his tea, but foolishly dropped it; he then hurried upstairs to his office, where he put the sceptre in a desk drawer just as the lights went on again. He then made for the Guard Room and pretended to be shocked at the discovery of the robbery.

His motive was simple. He believed that the sceptre held important clues to the whereabouts of other hidden tombs in Egypt, but that it would take much longer than the few months allowed to unravel the mystery. And he wanted to be the man who 'went down in history'. He did not think the Egyptians would allow many more expeditions because of what he called 'all this political nonsense', and wanted to make sure he was on the right track for further digs.

As Superintendent Browlee said, 'The professor may know a lot about the eating habits of the ancients, but when it comes to making a modern-day cup of tea, he has a lot to learn!'

PARTICLES OF DEATH

There are plenty of clues here for the hawk-eyed amateur detective. Here are a few:

The bottle that lay on its side behind the cellar door would point to someone being in the cellar. Only two people admitted to being in the cellar that evening—Keith Burnham and Penelope Miller. Given the times they said they were there, it would have been possible for them to knock out the cook and kill Bob Mason. And Burnham said he saw Penelope come out of the secret passage looking frightened—a fact she did not mention in her statement. Neither did she mention the car. Which is not surprising, because she did not hear it from the house—she was in fact on the upstairs floor looking for Peter Whitley. But Burnham heard it and saw it—driving *away* from the main gate. It was this fact which gave Sir Thomas his lead.

The clues above were 'red herrings'. The 'real' clues follow. But in order to understand their relevance, you should know who the guilty party was—assuming you have not already worked it out! The murderer of Bob Mason was none other than Peter Whitley, the security chief. And here's how Sir Thomas Rogers, ex-British Intelligence, worked it out.

For a start, Whitley said in his statement that he had never been in Sir Thomas's country house before. So how did he know that the buzzer was for the back door? When he said he followed Mason down to the hall, he made another stupid blunder: he claimed he heard Mason's 'footsteps going along the corridor'. But Dr Sedgewick had to go back for his slippers because the hall was not carpeted, which implies that the corridor, landing and stairs *were*—in which case it would have been impossible to hear footsteps.

Next, Whitley said he saw the car registration number (which he correctly identified as that of the cook's car) from the side window at the front door. Yet Penelope Miller said that she and Burnham went for a walk among the 'weeping willows' and the 'shaped hedges' on the front lawn. So it would have been impossible for Whitley to see any number.

But there were two things above all which told against Whitley's attempt to pin the blame on Karl Stevens. If Stevens had been driving the car, he couldn't have been in the house to take the telephone call! But it was the telephone call itself which was Whitley's really fatal mistake. Had Stevens been a spy, he would not have made an 'open' arrangement to meet his employers, in this case assumed to be Russian. He would have used a code, like 'My dear friend! How nice to hear from you! Have you just arrived in this country? And how's your wife—it's so long since I saw her!', and so on. This is known as double talk and means that an agent wants to meet his boss at a *pre-arranged* meeting place

Sir Thomas, having been in intelligence, knew all the ins and outs of double-talk. Whitley was presumably inexperienced in the field of national espionage as he had previously worked only in commercial security firms. This obvious lie on Whitley's part threw suspicion right back on himself. He was indeed in the pay of the Russians. He had driven the car out to the gate and handed it over to someone else, knocked out Stevens and killed Mason, who had threatened to expose him. The 'paper' was another red herring!

So as Sir Thomas said, all you had to do was use your intelligence!

NEPTUNE'S SECRET

First the clues to help you. The manservant seemed a suspect at the start. He said he had heard two arguments through the porthole. But Grant noticed the portholes looked out to sea. But remember, when Grant and the sergeant were in the cabin they heard the anchor fall on the deck and the shouting. In fact, the deck was above the cabin, so it *was* possible to hear conversations.

Secondly, Granger's symptoms. They could have shown arsenic poisoning, but they could have been just from a gastric disorder. Without adequate tests—which would be very difficult after Granger had been in the sea—it would be difficult to tell. And anyway, the fact that Granger was alive in the morning meant he could not have been killed by arsenic! At the most, he was being slowly poisoned, and the first dose had been given to him the night before.

The locker room provided further clues—the door was open. Did Patricia Granger open it for her 'close friend' Jonathan Bell? Were they both trying to get rid of Granger? And why did Bell say he was 'checking his gear' when he had no intention of diving? Again, all circumstantial evidence. Rafferty said he reached the locker 'about twenty past seven'—at least five minutes after Mrs Granger and Bell were there. She could have opened it for him (remember, she had a key), and he may have originally wanted to go diving.

But it was Bill Rafferty who gave the inspector the

answers he needed. Firstly, the fact that the air tanks had not been filled for two days meant at least two tanks were not full. There had been a squall the night before and all the tanks had been knocked to the floor. No one had his own individual set, and as Rafferty correctly pointed out it would be impossible to tell just from looking at the pressure or feeling the weights which tanks needed attention.

The answer then, well it looks as if Granger's death was a genuine *accident*. Rafferty had given him a half-empty tank by mistake. As Inspector Grant said, 'The secret was known by Neptune'. If it was murder there was certainly no proof that would hold up in court. Granger knew this. So . . . accidental death it was. Did you arrive at the same conclusion?

SMASH HIT

Working on two clues and one lie, Inspector Trent was able to pinpoint the murderer, Don Preston.

First of all, Chuck Watson told the detective that when he went along to Preston's dressing room the first time, the guitarist was sitting reading a book with his feet propped up on his locked guitar case. Yet when Chuck approached Preston the second time—only a few minutes before the concert—the guitarist was ready to go on. 'He picked up his guitar,' Chuck had said. Trent, from Barrett's evidence, knew that the guitar would need to be tuned. Had Preston not known anything about Bobby's death, he would have had to unlock his case and spend time tuning up.

Secondly, the glove was planted by Preston. When Barrett went to stuff his gloves in his coat pocket he must have dropped one, which was found by the guitarist. Preston wore it while stabbing Bobby. But Bobby was stabbed in the back and fell forward, so it would have been impossible for two fingers of the glove to be smeared with blood unless someone had deliberately rubbed it on. Which is what Preston had done, hoping Barrett would be blamed.

The lie Preston told was about hiding behind the partition. In fact he slipped up twice. Firstly, he said he went to see Bobby about 8.45. But Barrett had already said he had seen Bobby at 8.40 and had spent about 'five minutes' with him before leaving—a time which tallied with Richard Pease, the manager's evidence. But even if the men had been mistaken about the time, there was no way Don Preston could have hidden behind the partition without being seen: as the detective remembered, a mirror ran down the full length of the wall opposite the partition, making it quite impossible for anyone to hide.

Don Preston had hit the wrong chord when he tried to fool Inspector Trent.

A BLAST OF DEATH

Inspector 'Jock' Wilson arrested Alexander Newby and John Thorne. He charged Newby with murder and Thorne with conspiracy. At the subsequent court case, he was proven correct in his deduction.

Both men had made basic errors which the detective, although not a 'sporting man' was able to pick up. Newby, first of all, said Edward had taken Thorne's gun 'cracked the barrel' to see if it was loaded, and 'snapped it' straight again. Wilson knew no experienced gunhandler would walk through the countryside with a primed gun in firing position. This made the inspector suspicious. But when Alexander said he loaded his gun at the lodge, assuming the gamekeeper had extra cartridges, the detective's suspicions were confirmed. Alexander Newby knew he would have no need for extra cartridges.

Thorne's involvement in the murder became apparent when he said he left for the lodge and was gone 'only a few minutes' when he heard the blast from Sir Edward's gun. He claimed he ran back to the scene. But if he had he would have met the gamekeeper, who followed Thorne almost immediately. In fact, Thorne had waited behind a bush. That was why he was on the scene and able to carry Sir Edward's body back.

At the court case, it transpired that Thorne and Newby were trying to do a separate deal over the Middle East contract, one which would benefit them both and place Sir Edward in an embarrassing position.

As Alexander Newby said, the three brothers were always arguing, and Alexander wanted to take over the family business.

But all this came out later. Inspector Wilson worked only on the facts. As he said, 'It's amazing what you can uncover when you concentrate on the boring details.'

A SPEEDY END

Again, it's a question of picking up the right clues and tying them in with the overall story. And without wishing to disparage the police, Tom Mitchell had been right when he said they might have overlooked a few points.

It certainly looked as if David Blastow and Tessa Wright were prime suspects. He had been a mechanic and admitted to 'tinkering around' with bikes in his youth. And his story about his car breaking down seemed just *too* convenient. But would Tessa's knowledge about motor-bikes stretch to such detail about clutch-sprockets, even though she was meant to be an 'amazing lady' as Blastow said? Of course, when she tore her dress in the workshop she could have been kneeling by Groves's bike, but Tom doubted it.

Ted Marshall seemed a suspect at first after he had said he warned Bobby about 'something happening' to him if he didn't take life more seriously, and Tom had to admit that Marshall seemed the kind of man who would stop at nothing to make a point, especially after Marshall had said 'he (Bobby) might just have been hurt badly.'

And then, of course, we must not forget Count Vallère, from the opposition team, who was found coming out of the workshop with a spanner in his hand. And if anyone had a motive, he certainly had!

But it was the security guard who gave the game away. The notebook he gave Tom with the visitors in it had the guard's name and company written on the inside cover. Opposite, on the first page, were three names under the day, Saturday.

Now, the guard said he had been working on night shift watching the bike for five days. And yet, according to the book, he only started keeping records on Saturday—that's where the first page started. So obviously the book was made up *after* Saturday night, and there was no mention of the previous five nights.

Secondly, the guard stated he had a phone call from Ted Marshall, which he had to take in the main building. Two things were wrong here. Firstly, he had never met Marshall—Marshall hired the security firm, remember?— and so he could not be sure if it was the manager. (Luckily for him, by coincidence Marshall did phone twice, but on the second occasion the manager said it was his secretary who called.) Secondly, the guard said he had a small office. No security office would be without a phone, so why did he have to go to the main offices?

Thirdly, Bert Carter said he didn't know about machines and was a cyclist. And yet he was able to describe accurately the state of the bike after the accident, including information about the stem-head bolt, which he wouldn't have known about if he knew nothing about motor-bikes!

Lastly, David Blastow said he waved to the guard when he went in for the tools and then spoke to him when he returned them. Yet Bert's book only noted Blastow as appearing once. So it was Bert Carter who was the guilty party. Tom had no idea of the motive—that was for the police to find out in further questioning.

OFFICE PROCEDURE

The answer, of course, is that it was murder. Admitted it did *look* like suicide—especially after Parker had received the letter and the threat from his wife on the same morning.

Mitchell's story about a walk seemed suspicious, but that was not what gave Sergeant Webb his lead. There were a number of clues he picked up on which led him to the conclusion that Parker's death was *made* to look like suicide. Did you spot them? Here they are:-

Firstly, the position of Parker's body. If he had stabbed himself in the stomach, then he would have fallen forward. He was lying back, if you remember.

Secondly, the secretary, Miss Brown, said she waved to her friend in another building from the windows. That was impossible, as the blinds were down. (Remember, Webb asked for them to be opened?)

Thirdly, the secretary said she had tried to get through to New York most of the morning and finally reached it just before Mr Harris came in with his document. (Remember Harris's statement?) Then she said she had been lucky, because Mr Carboni was just leaving his office. But this had to be a lie: the time difference is six hours, which made the time in New York 4.30 am!

But the final piece of evidence for Webb before he arrested Miss Brown on a charge of murder was the 'blackmail' letter itself. It was dated the day before, and she said she had handed it to Parker herself. Which meant it was posted on Sunday. But as there are no collections on Sundays, the soonest the letter would have arrived would have been Tuesday.

In fact, Miss Brown had typed the letter herself and placed it in Parker's drawer. She had then killed him. As the police were to find out later, she was working for Carboni. Mitchell was in the clear, and his story, as it happens, was true.

And by the way, did you spot Miss Brown's other lie? She said she had typed a letter for Parker that morning, and he always insisted on fresh carbons. Well, when Webb and Stanstead went into her office they only found two envelopes in the waste-paper basket—no carbons.

Miss Brown, in making her office procedure look so efficient, had tried to be too clever—like most criminals.

THE FINAL CURTAIN

This fishy business behind the scenes contains a number of red herrings. Did you spot them? The argument with John Trent was one; Kate Osborne's statement was another; Lucy Arnold, the prompter, saying she had picked Osborne's knife up before he went on stage was yet another; and so was Kate Osborne's 'testing' of the knife.

With these out of the way, here are the real clues which pinpointed the culprit:

Firstly, the candle burning beside the rose gave Bond his first idea. You remember he sniffed the rose? And further, he picked up a small ball of grease which had fallen beside it. This meant that the grease had dripped down the left side of the candle, and that meant that a draught had come from the right—where the back door to the stage was situated. That was why Bond expressed an interest in the door.

But he had to find out who had left the door open long enough—approximately ten minutes, he reckoned—to allow the grease to fall. It was Debby Trent, the leading lady, who supplied the answer. She said she had gone in to take Osborne's picture and had done so with him leaning against his make-up counter. But there was a mirror behind the counter. No photographer, however amateur, would use flash directly into a mirror (remember the used flash bulb?). And then, she said he looked like an angel. *In his underwear*? (Remember Lucy

Arnold's story?) Hardly a picture for the scrap book! Bond realised this when Debby made another mistake—she said she helped him on with his costume, *after* taking the picture. And lastly, she said she could not stay in Osborne's dressing room because of the smell of paraffin which actors use in make-up. She was right that paraffin is used—but only to take make-up *off*.

So the murderess on the stage turned out to be the murderess in life. She had gone back to see Osborne after her husband had told her of his row with him. Osborne in fact had told her the previous night over dinner that he could not see her any longer and she planned the knife switch anyway.

As Bond said, it would have been better if they had been playing Macbeth. 'At least he wouldn't have had to be stabbed, but merely say, "Is this a dagger I see before me?' "

EQUATION OF MURDER

While there were three suspects with equally good motives, Brown was a good enough detective not to tie in motivation with an actual killing. He worked simply from clues which he picked up as each person told his tale. From that he was able to pinpoint Otto Wingarten as the murderer.

The first clue lay in the fact that Wingarten had said he had shot down from the top of the small hill. Yet the bullet which killed Professor Blumhoffen had entered his back, at the kidneys, passing through his heart and out of the body. In other words it had travelled *upwards*. If Wingarten's story was true, the bullet would have gone in the opposite direction.

Secondly, Wingarten said he watched the struggle with the 'dog' (which in fact wasn't in the woods at all) through his binoculars. This meant that the professor and the animal were too far away for him to view the scene clearly with the naked eye. Which meant in turn that he would have had to aim very carefully through his sights on the gun before shooting. Yet he said he was able to shoot immediately after watching the struggle between the mad dog and the professor through his glasses, which was impossible.

And thirdly, had Wingarten shot Blumhoffen from where he claims he was, the body would have fallen either to the side or backwards. Again, this contradicted the facts—the professor was found face down, stretched towards the centre of the clearing. Wingarten shot him from the woods.

His motivation was simple. He never forgave Blumhoffen for 'stealing' the Nobel Peace Prize, and although he tried to win Stella, decided that was not enough. In short, he was trying to be too clever with his story—but not clever enough.